The Type Righter

"From the opening narrative, author Rev. Dr. K. Helms piques the audience's attention while clutching their heart-strings. Just who is the Righter-and what is the communication's purpose? "Dream-time has reached its tipping point. Any movement towards getting back is futile." A feeling of urgency takes the reader over, each page snapping in anticipation; clarity and answers surely await on the next. . ."

Reverend Sharon Gordon MA

"Great story. Very allegorical with a good message for today's young adults. This is the kind of book you will want to not put down till you finish it."

Sue S.

The Type Righter

by
Rev. Dr. K. Helms

To my personal *Ze* who gives me healing
wings!

Table of Contents

PROLOGUE

CHAPTER 1 Beware of the Bird that Sings

CHAPTER 2 The Great Physician

CHAPTER 3 The Search for the Truth

CHAPTER 4 The Truth Shall Set You Free

CHAPTER 5 The Visit

CHAPTER 6 The Cipher

CHAPTER 7 Letter #1: The Signs

CHAPTER 8 Letter #2: The Wonders

CHAPTER 9 Letter #3: The Revelations

CHAPTER 10 The Plan

CHAPTER 11 The Release

CHAPTER 12 The Ruach

CHAPTER 13 The Rising

CHAPTER 14 The Quest

CHAPTER 15 The Name

EPILOGUE

Acknowledgement

Breathing life into this project would not have been possible without the relentless love and devotion of my husband Stan and my four adult children: Shayne, Jessie, Austin and Chase. They never stopped believing in me.

Much appreciation goes to my son Chase who spent hours with me encouraging me. He was my voice of reason and understanding for the cover design.

Editing was metamorphic! Tribute goes to several sources. My lovely daughter Jessica Thaxton Helms shared her time, and talent dedicating hours to the process. Linda Miller shared her insights, and wisdom. Much appreciation also goes to a wonderful group of women who without hesitation lovingly invited me in expressing a genuine interest in my writing endeavor. They served as my beta readers during a time that I really needed to take the leap, and put myself out there. Thank you for choosing to catch me and not let me fall.

Because of the nature of my novel it is very important that I acknowledge my own courage to be my true self. Yes! Writing is that much a part of me, and instead of hiding it or being afraid, I am at a point in my healing journey to completely embrace who God has made me to be. I am so appreciative of the healing qualities of writing. It has taught me about myself; how to truly love myself! Why is it so hard you might ask? Because I know as a writer the words on the page are not just words on a page, but a deep part of my very being. I thank the writing for being my greatest teacher of self-love.

Prologue

NOTE TO READER: I know it may seem this letter has appeared from nowhere, and I assure you THAT is not the case; this letter has surely appeared from somewhere! It is imperative that you take into consideration the importance and urgency of its prophetic qualities. Heed these words of warning! Be assured that my efforts to reach out to you are for reasons beyond biblical proportion. Your decision to believe what I'm telling you, and the power of the narrative to compel you to action in your present state, is at its most desirable point in the history of time and space to make a difference.

I wish I could reveal to you my true-identity, but if I were to do that in the written word I would surely be found out and immediately annihilated. Thus, my power to tell the story with the chance of my voice being heard would be like the only flicker of a candle's flame in a stark black room being snuffed out by the breath of darkness. It is a risk I'm willing to take. My hope is that you will not only hear what I am about to share with you but will listen so closely to the whispers of enlightenment that you discover and experience it along the way. My hope is that you will recognize *MY* living truth as a shared truth that belongs to both of us.

Although my ability to share explicitly is limited, I can share with you that this letter is one that has been written in the future. It has appeared to you in what I consider my historical past by means that may be hard for you to understand. Let's just say in your historical period, the aboriginal people of Australia understand the ability of *Alcheringa* or dream-time. In the future, we have mastered the power of dream-time, have it at our disposal, and use it in all sorts of capacities.

Alcheringa is my only saving grace in my ability to communicate with you. It would be to my detriment to reveal my identity. If In the telling of my tale you can figure out who I am, then, you will discover your biggest help and companion for your life's calling. Let me leave you now with this warning: The worst kind of disillusionment is the kind that you slowly wake up to and realize that what once seemed real is nothing but smoke and mirrors. Be cautious of the slow turnings that are hard to put your finger on, but you know exist because you sense them in your gut. Beware of the false prophets that come like saving angels. If you have ears, listen!

BEWARE OF THE BIRD THAT SINGS!

"Then I saw 'a new Heaven and a new Earth
for the first Heaven and the first Earth had
passed away. . ."
(NIV, Rev. 21:1)

I know you must still be in shock and second guessing yourself about the appearance of this letter. However, I implore you to place your devotion on its content more than how it got into your possession. It is of utmost importance that I share with you what I know to be true of future events. That is- What is your future but serves as my present.

I assure you it will be detrimental to all humanity if you do not take me seriously. Also, I want you to know that the conditions under which I'm able to communicate are very difficult at best. At any time, I might be interrupted, and I would have to come back when another opportunity lends itself; not to blow my cover. Please! Listen carefully to what I share with you, and once the story is told, I am confident you will do the right thing! Even though I cannot reveal my true-identity, I will refer to myself as the Type Righter. Kind of a play on words, wouldn't you say? Ironic, since I use a typewriter as my only way of communicating with you. This is my way of trying to make the course of history *right* itself.

Under the guise of night, I have a better chance of not getting caught. My only hope in this process is not to be found out.

I must trust that you are truly on the other end reading what I have sent. I have no way of knowing. . .

....

The environment in which I currently live is known as the new Heaven and the new Earth. That may sound strange to you but know that it was created after the battle of Armageddon in 2100 A.C.E. because of the mass destruction of the old Earth in which you currently live. We now refer to our time in history as N.H.E. (time of the new Heaven and Earth).

Lead scientists decided to design the new Earth with less of a gravitational pull. One advantage to this idea is the development of different ways of transport. For example, most people don't walk in the traditional sense that you are used to. In fact, most people float just slightly above the ground with inertia of some kind. People can propel themselves in any direction; even fly if they want to. This one change in physics has created a "hay day" for inventors and consumers in the public venue. This was a great move on the part of the scientists to boost the economy of the new Heaven and Earth.

This change alone has helped me exorbitantly! In a society where someone like me is trying to keep my anonymity, I don't have to worry so much about leaving my footprints or DNA behind! This gives me an advantage to keep my enemies close, and even be in their presence without their suspicion. This leads me into the part of the narrative where I introduce you to some of the characters at play and my current disposition.

....

    I made it a point on this day to blend in with the crowd as much as possible. The street that led up to the town square spilt over with people. There was excitement in the air that ignited like electricity. The anticipation of seeing the Mashiach whose name was Aadah Nakal was hard to contain. Seeing the Messiah of the world, the High Priestess of the new world religion was such a rare occurrence. I saw this as one of the only opportunities to make my way into the Temple mound. I hid behind one of the large, beautifully textured glass trees that lined both sides of the street in anticipation of my next move.

    Normally, people had the freedom on any given day to transport as high into the air as they would like but not in the presence of Mashiach of the N.H.E. (new Heaven and Earth) In the presence of the High Priestess, only she could stand the tallest amongst all the people. Aadah Nakal would be presented before the crowd on a special platform carried on the shoulders of four Temple monks. The ascending stage arched upward and was made of pure gold.

    Following behind her in a parade-like fashion were some of the most important world leaders. Peppered amongst her followers were the life feeders, Aadah's entourage of faithful worshippers. Expectedly, I had hoped to see the likes of Ophis Phineus. My body shuddered at the thought of seeing him. If he ever caught wind of my being close in proximity to the High Priestess or to him, I surely would not be in existence to write this to you.

Suddenly, a wash of silence hushed over the crowd. I peered carefully from behind the iridescent branches of the beautifully artistic, glass street-sculptures I hid behind. From this vantage point, I saw and heard a familiar sight. Flittering its wings with hastened intent, a Pitohui caught my eye. The black-hooded sprite of a bird donned its orange-yellow, striped mid-belly and landed as gracefully as an angel in the branch above my head. With stillness in the air and in the hush of human anticipation, the little bird opened its beak. The feathered spirit began trilling a melodious, magical tune that lulled the crowd into a drugged stupor. As I witnessed what was happening, anger bubbled up into my throat. Almost zombie-like, all the people dropped to their knees, prostrate before Aadah Nakal, known as the Mashiach or Messiah of the second coming. Being unaffected by the entrancing song, I continued to observe the approaching sycophants from behind the tree of life.

Was I dreaming? There before me was the Messiah Aadah Nakal who approached in all her glory. I must admit my knees buckled for a moment. However, I resisted the urge. She was breath-taking! Standing over six feet tall, her thin, pale skin only accentuated her "deer-like" innocent qualities. Her pursed lips and small features were contrasted by her large, mesmerizing eyes.

On the rare occasion that the Mashiach,

High Priestess appeared in public, Aadah was always seen in her vestments. I had never witnessed her in person before, and I was awe-struck. Aadah Nakal's elaborate headdress and tightly fitted garments were made entirely of gold coins. Underneath her royal armor, wisps of a white robe could be seen. Draped around her right ankle was tied a glistening golden cord that trailed out from under her robe, across the raised platform, and was held by the devoted parade of adoring life feeders as they chanted repeatedly, "Adira! Adira!" with admonition of her nobility and power.

In her presence, there are two close confidants who are always by her side. One whose job is to protect and advise the Mashiach is Counselor Modsiw. At the distance from which I was standing, it was hard for me to catch a glimpse of her. The best possible chance to get a glimpse is to stare at Aadah Nakal's ear because this is where High Counselor Modsiw hovers with her fairy-like wings to whisper words of counsel into the Priestess's ear. Counselor Modsiw is better seen at night, so I'm told because of her glow. It is my understanding that the voice of the Mashiach is so sacred, Aadah Nakal will use the voice of Counselor Modsiw to express her wishes to the crowd. So, even though Counselor Modsiw is tiny, her voice is large and "God-like" when she addresses the people on behalf of Aadah Nakal. This is only the first of characters that is always seen with the Mashiach. The second, I also observed on this day.

As the High Priestess was approaching in closer proximity to where I was standing,

5

I caught a quick glimpse of "Ubu", whom she caressed and carried lovingly in her left hand. "Ubu" is a reference I make to her Majesty's famous companion that travels with her wherever she goes. In our day and age, science has advanced to the point that pets are custom-made to our liking; part DNA manipulation, part computer chip. In this case, Chava of the N.H.E (Aadah Nakal's other title) is never seen without her miniature, brindle, long-haired chipet, "Ubu". I heard that Aadah Nakal detests barking. Because of this, she customized "Ubu" to purr like a cat instead. She is reported in a paper I read as saying, "Barking is so crass and chaotic! Purring only promotes peace and harmony!" I guess this reflects the fulfillment of her role as "Princess of Peace" as the chronicles had prophesied. I wish you could see my face as I type this. At the thought of the scene, I can only muster a sarcastic, cynical snicker.

My amusement was short-lived because in that moment I heard the voice of Ophis Phineus barking orders to the High Priestess' attendants. My blood started to curdle. Fear gripped every cell in me. My first instinct was to run. However, my body only stood motionless; frozen in place.

"You need to keep the line moving! The people only need a glimpse of her, not a full display that might put her Majesty in danger! Now move it along!"

The agitation in Ophis' voice just heightened the uneasiness in me like fingernails on a chalkboard. (This statement is giving you a hint to my age because chalkboards only existed on the old earth. This world is too advanced, and most people don't even know what one is!) But Phineus would know because he comes from the world before the N.H.E., and remembers the way the world used to be. He is legendary because he survived the battle of Armageddon. He has been highly rewarded for his scientific advancements especially those that brought about the development of the new Heaven and the new Earth. He's a smooth operator, and I'm not convinced that all his advancements have been for the good of humanity.

Phineus is one of the most influential world leaders, and holds the position of Chief Scientist at the Bureau of the New World Order. Let's just say he wears his riches on his sleeves. Most people in my society covet his svelte, clean cut, European flare. Playing the part of the spoiled "only child" that he is, he stands out as a key figure not only in the present but in our past. I've learned to be wary of those who are held up so highly and are given too much power. It only means that powerlessness for someone else remains.

Knowing that Phineus was near just meant I needed to be extra careful. His presence didn't change my plans to find a way into the Temple. With Ophis Phineus at the front of the entourage, I looked for an opportunity without being detected. At the exact moment when Phineus wasn't looking, and the back of her Holiness had passed me, I quickly blended in with the life feeders holding the golden cord that was attached to Aadah's royal ankle. I chanted along with them, "Adira! Adira!"

Just before I fully committed to what I

was about to do my eyes followed the flight of the hooded bird as it made its way to lightly land on Ophis Phineus's shoulder. I quickly slipped my way underneath the canopy of the golden stand that held the Anointed One, Aadah Nakal. If the crowd had not been lulled by the Pitahui's melodious song, I am sure I would have been noticed by someone in the crowd.

Once underneath, it was important for me to keep in step and rhythm with the four monks carrying her Highness. It was strange to be walking with my feet touching the ground in complete darkness, and not be able to see where I was going. To insure allegiance and respect to the Mashiach, anyone within twenty subsets of the Messiah could only transport by walking with their feet touching the ground. This was Aadah Nakal's power over those closest to her that defied the lack of gravity. The crowd's response was always astonishment when seeing the Mashiach's ability to affect those around her in this way because it was like seeing Jesus walk on water! Even though I was not acclimated to this new feeling of human flesh touching the earth, I held my breath that this would be my way into the most, holiest place on Earth, the Temple mound.

Why would I take such a huge risk on my life? I wanted to know what was really going on. This was the only way I knew how to get a taste of the truth from the inside. I needed a glimpse of the world's organizations at play, all in one place, paying homage to Aadah Nakal, or so it seemed. . . I soon found out. . . oh, shoot! Someone's coming! I've got to go for now. . .

....

    I apologize for my quick exit when I
last made contact with you. It is very
important that I not be found out. I haven't
shared with you up to this point the reason
I have been able to stay under the radar,
and get information to you. I know you are
aware that I write to you via typewriter.
However, what I have not told you is that my
discovery of this vintage typewriter has
kept my efforts undetectable in my culture
because of its *lack* of technology. If I were
to choose another source to contact you,
(and believe me there are advancements you
haven't even heard of) it would surely be
detected by the powers that be. Scientific
technology has grown to such proportions
that most of everyday life is monitored,
evaluated, and documented. This typewriter
is my salvation and my life-line to you! I
hope it proves as a greater salvation for
the larger world. Let me gather my thoughts
and return to the narrative. . .Now let me
see, where was I?

....

    Although I could not see because of
being in the darkness, hiding underneath
Aadah Nakal's Messianic pedestal, I did the
best to perk my listening skills, and the
result? I felt a heightening of my other
senses. I was extremely aware of the
changing texture under my feet from smooth,
hot pavement, to the irregular tapestry of
stones affecting my balance. This

9

irregularity gave a hint that we were nearing the front doors to the outer gates of the Temple. The caravan stopped for a moment, and I heard the rushing forward of running feet, along with the mumbling of voices. I could feel the balance of weight changing above my head. Without warning the long, curved legs of her Majesty's carrying apparatus made the sound of a giant sonic boom. As the monks stepped away, the ornate platform fell bluntly to the ground; coming to a screeching halt. This maneuver startled me so much that my claustrophobia kicked in. Stuck in what felt like a darkened tomb, I realized no one knew where I was.

"Deep breathe! Deep breathe!" I told myself again and again. I decided to concentrate on what was happening outside of my new acquired predicament instead of feeling like a caged animal.

From what I could gather, Counselor Modsiw must have been addressing the crowd on behalf of the Mashiach because the four cloth walls that surrounded me began to tremble, and vibrating with decibels of sound emitted by Counselor Modsiw's "God-like" voice. Although I could not make out every word, I did catch a phrase or two of what was being said to the people:

"Remember me! I am the life-giver of all. . . Take to memory all I have taught you. . . Let the results of Armageddon be a warning to wear the Word in your heart ONLY!"

Although the roar of the crowd sounded far away, the closer sensation of heavy, creaking, and groaning of wood on metal gave signal that the gateway doors were opening. The Mashiach was about to enter the Temple, and many people over the centuries thought this sacred site would never come to fruition. My heart was thumping so hard I thought someone would hear it and discover me as a stowaway.

I was startled when I felt a burst of cold air fly up from underneath the draped walls that surrounded me. A slit of light shone at my feet indicating the caravan was about to move forward on the shoulders of the monks again.

I wish I could describe to you the thrill of excitement just to know my destination was the inner sanctum. I could not believe I was pulling this off without detection. The only hint we were crossing the outer courts was the cobble stones beneath my feet and the smoky smell of burning sage in the air. Part of the tradition left over from the old Earth is to use fire to illuminate the path to the main Temple. Fire to us seems antiquated. I had only heard rumors of this ceremony of illumination. I could not believe I was present experiencing it firsthand.

Ascending an uncountable number of stairs that challenged my balance, I did everything I could not to trip and fall. Frequently I felt my way on all fours. It was music to my ears to feel the vibration of the sounding shofar that tingled my nerves in anticipation of entering the inner court.

Once inside, I could tell the immensity of the space because every sound echoed. It reminded me how careful I would need to be not to draw attention to myself. I poked my head out from under the pedestal, low to the ground, to get my bearings. I realized the room was completely dark which would hide my identity. I quietly crept from underneath my protective "Trojan horse" to blend in with the others standing in the sacred space of the Temple.

An attendant instructed us to put on one of the shrouds hanging on the wall behind me. I quickly put one on to cover my entire body not to be noticed or stand out from the crowd. Built into these strange looking suits were high-tech eye gear resembling goggles. Counselor Modsiw explained, "It is imperative that you wear the sacred shroud to ensure no one comes into direct contact with the Holy Spirit of the living God." After slipping on my new disguise, the room took on a reddish hue.

I wondered why I felt disoriented, and could not put my finger on it at first. With closer inspection, I realized looking through my goggles, the walls of the Temple were holographic. Different scenes were depicted on them to induce a worshipful state. During this stage of ceremonial rites, I scanned the room to see if I could determine where Ophis Phineus was standing. Wearing a shroud with tinted goggles along with the holographic images made me feel like I was at a masquerade ball. I felt safer in the moment not knowing where Phineus was.

The beauty of the holograms is beyond my grasp to describe to you. It was

completely mesmerizing, almost intoxicating.
This display seemed to empty the mind, and
pour into it tranquility. The room went to
pitch black darkness. Looking up, I saw a
glimpse of light that started the size of a
pen-point. Descending slowly, the ember
floated towards me. Suddenly, one light
split into many, multiplying like a cell.
There were stars resembling the Pleiades
that danced above my head like glittering
flickers of light. I envisioned their motion
as feathers streaming slowly downward. Then
I realized each glow was a candle finding
its owner; one eventually gracing the grip
of my hand.

    With the illumination of the room, I
could now see what surrounded me. Reflecting
the light, I saw each wall made of pure
black polished marble. They were etched with
the names of ancestors from the old Earth;
those who gave their lives during the third
world war. Beautiful arches, stretching
from floor to ceiling, encased three-
dimensional stained glass windows. Each pane
was made of multicolored hexagons and
pentagons forming hundreds of truncated
icosahedrons. As I looked more closely, I
noticed each spherical ball held a moving
hologram either with a figure quoting a
remembered scripture or an instrument
playing beautiful music. One cluster
portrayed angel-like beings with fluttering
wings. I looked over and noticed Counselor
Modsiw glowing with a thought of pleasure.
She had wings in common with these
holographic adornments of the Temple. By the
look on her tiny face I could tell she was

in her element, with Aadah Nakal by her side in faithful service to her whispered wisdom.

I was so transfixed in the moment that my mind slowly came to an awareness of an altar table that had been there the whole time in front of Aadah Nakal. Distracted, I had scarcely noticed it. I sensed a chill go up my spine as I anticipated that something was about to happen. What signaled a sinking feeling in my stomach was the fact that the life-feeders began to chant a rhythmic, hypnotic tune as they began, almost robotically, encircling the sacrificial altar.

In the periods of silence, between the sung notes of the life-feeders, I could hear the juxtaposition of peaceful purring coming from the inner cloak pocket of the High Priestess. Ubu, with an air of an uncaring spirit with what was happening, was curled into a ball fast asleep snuggled against the rib cage of the Holy one.

In that instant, the High Priestess raised her right hand up towards the heavens, and our eyes followed the suggested point of her finger. Streaming downward in liquid motion, a long crimson cloth flowed towards us. Aadah Nakal uttered some sort of summons, and a figure got closer; gracefully landing on the altar piece. It was a human being!

Aadah Nakal laid hands on the figure's forehead as if delivering a blessing. However, the tone in her voice sounded more ominous. She proceeded to peel back the facial veil revealing the individual's identity. I could not believe my eyes! It was all I could do not to let out a scream of protest. My nerves, caused by my silent screams, created beads of sweat to form on my forehead and drip into the recesses of my goggles. I thought I was going to be sick.

There in front of me lay one of the most prolific and political writers of my time. I have read just about everything she has ever written; much of her writing following the journey of Aadah Nakal's reign. My brain and my heart were slowly waking up to the reality of why we were here.

I whispered her name, but not too loudly, "Thusia!"

Thusia has been so valuable to the cause. She is one of the only ones like me left in the N.H.E. I felt so helpless standing there watching the whole scene unfold, and I was powerless to do anything about it.

"Do you have any last words?" the High Priestess asked with a strained tone.

In defiance, Thusia took from her crimson robe a scroll and proceeded to unroll it. With a confidence that reflected the conviction in her written words, she uttered for the last time:

"The written word is Word in flesh. Human flesh enables the written word. One cannot argue what is seen on the page, but one can argue what one remembers. May the generations who fought for freedoms of expression before me, and those who continue the fight after me, prevail above all powers that be to suppress them."

I felt the coldness of a tear run down

my face.

Out of my left peripheral vision, I caught the glimpse of the Pitahui taking flight, and reflecting the light of the candles off its oily sheen that seemed to drip from its wings. Thusia locked her eyes on the enchanting sight. She seemed to be in a trance like state. Mesmerized, she reached out, and lovingly embraced the ornithological creature in her hands. She smiled as the bird began to sing a dirge. As she cupped her hands close to the bird's body, the feathered beauty draped its heavy-laden wings tightly around the outside of her hands like a blanket.

With every touch of the skin, Thusia exposed herself to the injecting toxins emitted by the melodious bird.

"Why is it the most beautiful must also be the deadliest?" I dreadfully thought. My mind reeled uncontrollably and then sank with her last breath. . .

Now you see why I must get my story out to you. It is all about the silence; the silencing of the voice, *the written voice.*

It is forbidden.

They will come for me. . .

THE GREAT PHYSICIAN

"Sometimes one tires of being a mirror
without reflection. . ." (Dr. K. Helms)

I had intentionally slipped to the back
of the crowd in the room. Instinctually, I
picked up the silky end of the golden cord
along with the other life feeders to blend
in. Knowing it was attached to the right
ankle of the Mashiach, I felt a little
empowered in that moment with the thought
that I was literally holding onto a device
that with one swift jerk could trip up the
most influential, powerful figure of our
time.

As I witnessed the Messiah enter the
Holy of Holies, I realized all eyes would
fall on her, and I could make my escape. In
that moment, I noticed a swift shimmer of
light emitting just beyond an archway that
caught my attention. Even though it was
dark, my eyes saw a glimpse of a reflection
off of a mysterious woman's glasses. I had
not noticed her there before. As I moved in
that direction towards her I heard the
familiar voice of Ophis Phineus being
projected from the opposite side of the
room.

With agitation, and a sense of wanting
to be in control, Phineus barked, "Hey,
where are you going?"

My attention quickly shifted to the
figure I had first noticed in the archway.
My body went into flight mode, and without
thinking I started to run toward the
shimmering speck of light I had seen

earlier. With all my defenses raised like a caged animal, I tried to find my way out. I heard steps rushing behind me which caused my heart and breathing to quicken. Before I knew it, I was running, but not in the traditional sense of the word. When I ran past the archway into the hallway, I began running in the air! It dawned on me that I must be outside the perimeters of subsets. The Mashiach's influence of power was not in effect anymore. Without any friction on the ground beneath my feet, and no way really to transport outside the confines of the building, all I knew to do was use my feet to kick off the sides of the walls to work my way upward towards the ceiling so as not to be noticed. As I rose higher I hesitated to look down. (Not because of being afraid of heights which I assure you I am not). My biggest fear came true when I peered down and saw a figure standing below me. I squeezed my eyes shut repeating to myself, "It's only a dream! It's only a dream!" When I finally peeked through my lenses, there below me stood a dark figure looking to and fro as if trying to discern which direction I had gone down the multiple corridors.

"It must be Phineus!!!" I thought with panic. In my one last effort to ascend higher, I miscalculated, and my head hit the edge of a stone gargoyle protruding outward from the ornate cathedral-like ceiling. All I remember is the sensation of wind beating against my shroud and everything fading to black. . .

This is where I'd like to introduce you to

Dr. Rebekah Muse. . .

"Tell me, what happened?" I asked Dr. Muse feeling the pain in the top of my head.

"All I know is," she said, "when I peeked into the room, I saw you running towards me. I quickly hid behind one of the Temple statues as you ran by. I stepped back into the archway and there was Ophis Phineus asking in an angry voice, 'Did you see where that life feeder went?'"

"At first I tried to convince Phineus that his participation in the Temple ritual was more important. The Mashiach would surely notice his absence. But he just would not have it. He was so persistent. With a slight movement of my hand, I adjusted the right corner of my glasses simultaneously setting them up on my nose and pressing a hidden button within the frame which sprayed a neuro-inhibitor that affects memory directly into his face. He froze in time, did a double-take, and said in a pleasant voice, 'Dr. Muse, I do not remember why I came this way. I was looking for something, but can't quite remember what!' I assured him, 'I actually overheard you telling one of your colleagues you were going to look for the anointing oil for the ceremonial rites.'

'Oh yes, that's right!'

'They are over there in the canonical cabinet,' I responded as naturally as possible.

'I appreciate your help and by the way Muse, keep up the excellent work!'"

Rebekah continued. "Once I had him redirected, my curiosity was bubbling over.

Quite honestly, this is where my adrenaline kicked in trying to find you.I was the one you saw in the hallway. I would not have even known to look up to find you accept for the grotesque moan you let out after hitting your head. Because your shroud acted as a type of flying suit, your rate of fall was slowed. Knowing you had no risk of hitting the ground due to being in the anti-gravity zone, I maneuvered my transport in such a way to catch you on your descent. Since you were hovering, I just pulled you along behind me and brought you to my private lab. Don't worry. No one knows you are here." She reassured me.

....

    It was at this point I started to notice my surroundings. My first sensation was how comfortable I was in my levitating cocoon bed that I had seen in many advertisements, and knew it as the "C500". I had heard about these. However, experiencing one was very comforting. I found that as I adjusted my body in any direction the cushioned surface below me would adjust with my weight. There were cool colored lights built into the bed that measured all my vital signs which eliminated the need for loud beeping machines. By verbal command, I could request soothing music that would play near my ears no matter where my head lay on the bed. Because my head was pounding, I was not in the mood for music. Even aroma therapy was an option. I decided to test the commands, "C500, lavender scent, please!" A

soft soothing spray fell gently on my body
like a mist, and my nerves were calmed by
the sweet fragrance of the pale purple
flower.

I remembered having quite the headache
though. My mind was spinning trying to
decipher who this Dr. Muse was, and whether
I could trust her or not. I'm sure she was
thinking the same about me, especially since
I very obviously was in such a highly
prestigious holy place uninvited for reasons
she was unaware.

In that moment, Dr. Muse injected,
"Right now, your job is to rest. We can talk
more, later." She placed her hand on my
chest. Her facial features were soft and
welcoming like an attentive mother. Shortly,
she blurred out of focus and I drifted into
unconsciousness. . .

....

When I awoke, I remember feeling more
sluggish than normal. My pulse was weak and
I had an aching that would not stop. Dr.
Muse entered the room, "You must be
famished. I brought you some delicious
treats to get your strength back."

"I feel like everything is underwater."
I said, trying to get my bearings. "I don't
have much of an appetite."

"Well, you just lie down and relax.
With our advancements, not much is required
of you. Working in the Pharmaceutical field,
I helped develop the concept of portable
medicinal foods that were used in the
transition from the old Earth to the new

Earth. My food product has been used to sustain the lives of millions of people especially during the time of the Great War. So, I would say you landed in the hands of the right woman."

I felt her gently take my arm in her hands. Where my elbow was bent, she straightened my arm. Dr. Muse then proceeded to carefully stick to the soft fleshy inside part of my arm what looked like clear gel-filled medical patches. She named each one.

"For your pain, I offer a combination of pain-inhibitors with chocolate, and for your strength a protein punch of filet mignon. Would you like to finish your meal off with warm, buttery mashed potatoes, carbohydrates mixed with a bit of relaxant for the nerves?"

With each application, I not only had the sensation of the taste in my mouth but I could smell the luscious food that made for a wonderful experience in my brain. The mouth-watering flavors lasted unexpectedly on my tongue as if I were savoring a fancy meal at a high-end restaurant.

At last I felt the effects of the relaxant. Before drifting back to sleep, she must have made an impression on me because I remember saying, "This must be our first date."

....

Several days had passed. It was time to test the waters to see if Dr. Muse would help me on my further mission. I was feeling much stronger now.

Over the past few days, she was so kind

and nurturing. She would certainly not deny the information I needed in my quest. I could not imagine the scenario any other way. Come to think of it, Dr. Muse didn't even ask who I was or what I was doing at the Temple in the first place. Maybe she didn't have to ask. Maybe, she already knew. This thought caused a wave of uneasiness to bubble to the surface.

"Dr. Muse, you have cared for me so graciously over the past few days. Your bedside manner is impeccable. However, I am curious why you have not asked me about my presence in the Temple or why I was trying to get away."

She carefully listened and responded in kind, "Let's just say, I've been on the inside for a long time. I know what goes on here. Anyone trying to run and get away from it must be okay in my book. Your actions speak louder than any words to me you could say."

I asked further, "Dr. Muse, did you know Thusia?"

"Oh, please call me Rebekah. First let me say, I am sorry for your pain in the loss of your friend. You must still be in shock over her murder. It is hard for me to show my outrage, but be assured that I am. Let's just say I knew of her. I'm very fond of her work. Her writings have inspired so many people. Please don't let the Mashiach or Ophis Phineus for that matter hear me saying these words. It would be treason." She expressed herself very matter-of-factly.

I pressed her a little bit more, "Perhaps then you might know where I could find Thusia's work. I am aware the remnants have been preserved, I just don't know where."

"What remains of her writing can be found at the Science Archeological Library in Melpomene where all the artifacts from old Earth are on display. Since high security is needed to access any of the items, and I am considered to have high security clearance, I think I'm your ticket in."

"Why are you so willing to help me?" I said not knowing whether to trust her or not.

"Even though not everything I do seems to your benefit or comfort, it is to your advantage to trust me."

In some strange way, I didn't feel so alone in that moment. A well of emotions flooded to the surface, and reality struck that this was only the beginning of an adventure that was going to transform my life. I had to dive in, all or nothing.

The SEARCH FOR THE TRUTH

"Sometimes things aren't always what they
seem . . ."

I started to feel detached from my
body. When I looked up, I could see a
ghostly hue of my essence hanging above my
head.
"This is only for precaution purposes."
Rebekah yelled from behind me in competition
with the loud humming that vibrated the
whole room.
She continued, "Now, stand still just a few
more seconds."
Rebekah, holding what looked like a
tiny movie camera with laser lights shooting
from it, meticulously scanned my body up and
down until the hologram was complete.
With a sigh of relief, she spoke in a
normal tone. "This will come in handy for
getting what we want at the archeological
library."
Her statement made me think that
accessing the S.A.L. wasn't going to be as
easy as Dr. Muse had first made it out to
be.

....

The day finally arrived.
"So, Rebekah, what would you suggest as
the best way to transport for our mission
today?" I said in a hurry to get started.
Rebekah seemed preoccupied with the morning
routine. She chimed back from the other
room, "I have three choices: the hover-
board, hover shoes or the H-pack. The hover-

board is cool, and great for outdoor transport. However, we would have to carry the hover-boards in our arms or find a place for them; not very practical for a secret mission. I vote for the hover shoes over the H-pack. Not only are they stylish, they are also my favorite way to transport. They have an advantage over the H-pack because they are quiet; not emitting a sound. I must emphasize that the technology has not quite been perfected with the backpack inertia system. Hover shoes have been around for a long time."

"Hover shoes get my vote!" I chimed in as I started to put them on. I was anxious to get started. I was feeling like my old self again. After being cooped up in a bed for so long, I was ready to continue my journey with Dr. Muse's help.

We had transported quite a distance, passing many buildings. The outdoor sounds were so inviting and full of energy. It was not unusual to observe a robot almost on every corner trying to sell some bangle or bobble. My favorites were the robotic feeding stations. The smell of slow cooked Zezublé wafted past my nose as we rounded the next corner. I imagined it melting on my tongue, and my stomach grumbled in response. Rebekah startled me from my foodie stupor. "We are here!"

I looked around not seeing any evidence of the library. But I did notice the children on the playground across the street. With my short attention span, I was immediately drawn back to my childhood.

....

I am sure what I am about to describe to you is different from any playground you have ever seen. However, I assure you it is so much fun. I wish you could travel to the future, in my time, and have the joy of experiencing child-play in anti-gravity. Let's just say parents don't have to worry about their children falling. You are probably curious about what a playground in the future looks like. Here are a few descriptions of play equipment I saw on this play yard. I enjoyed many of these myself when I was younger.

The first I'll describe is a pole with a rope attached at the top with a rotation hook. I think on old Earth we had something similar that held a ball at the end of the rope. With anti-gravity, instead of a ball, there is a handle that is held by the participant. A friend then gives a good push, and the child's whole body will fly around the pole.

For the more athletic individuals, the Duostele (pronounced: Do-oh-stee-lay) is the way to go. This was one of my favorites growing up. It looks quite simple, and consists of two rectangles standing upright parallel to each other. Each is made from a trampoline material. Those who are very experienced put their transports at a high inertia setting, and bounce off from one side to the other doing complicated flips in the middle of the air.

I know in your understanding the tallest playground equipment is probably the sliding board. We have something similar yet different. Remember there is no possibility of a child hitting the ground. Let's just say, things have gotten taller or higher in the air to intensify the thrill factor. Also, transport allows children to fly high in the air (with adult supervision, of course). Imagine a slide hanging in midair and cut into three pieces. The first part is a huge hill that a child slides down with the end tilted upward. The child is then catapulted about five feet in old Earth terms and faithfully caught by the next piece of the slide. A predictable "Weeee!" is heard by children on the third leg of the slide that is shaped in a spiraling cylinder. The further down the cylinder, the faster the child is spit out at the end. This is done with such speed that without brakes built into the front of their inertia shoes, they would just keep going with nothing to stop them. I find it comical to not just watch the faces of the children, but also the expressions on the faces of the parents who in dread hold their breath and then give a sigh of relief. As adults, how much we forget the freedom from worry children possess.

Do you remember rock climbing walls? We have something very similar. The equipment is designed more after the old vintage video games. In the future, there are no walls to climb, there are only hover disks in the sky arranged in different levels. The kids climb them, and strategize using their inertia shoes and sheer climbing strength.

....

"Hello, anybody home?" Rebekah chided while poking my side. Evidently, I had been daydreaming looking in the direction of the playground.

"Well . . ." I said, "Where is it?"

"It is not so obvious and quite undetectable with first perceptions, unless you are looking for it." she said reminding me of its high security.

As was true of some of the surrounding buildings, decorations could be found donning some of the comforts of old Earth just for sentimental purposes. The objects of remembrance held no real function or so it seemed. We came upon a building squeezed tightly between two other structures. It was only.oo5 subset in width although it stood very tall. (In old Earth terms, about twelve inches in width). At about chest height was a round metal disk painted blue with a small handle on it. As I got closer, I noticed the words "U.S. Mail" stamped on it. This was a dinosaur from the past; a remembrance for old time's sake. I say this because mail has not been in existence for the past four hundred plus years.

"Things aren't always what they seem!" Rebekah said with a sly grin. I'm going in."

"What do you mean going in?" I said slightly confused.

"This is my portal into the library!"

"There is no way you are fitting in that thing. Besides, how does such a tiny building hold such a storehouse of archeological treasures?"

She responded with an air of knowing in her voice. "This building was built as part of the Alcheringa Project. It was constructed in dream-time. The outside façade hides the true-identity to preserve

it, and not cause un-do attention to it.
Believe me, I've done this many times
before. Do you see that playground over
there? I want you to find a spot, and wait
for me there." My excitement melted down my
body and landed at my feet.

"Hey wait a minute! I thought I was
going in with you?" I said with
disappointment in my voice.

"Well, you are. . .sort of. Here, put
these on."

In that moment, she slipped a pair of
glasses over my ears and on the bridge of my
nose. These weren't just any ordinary
glasses. They had an active computer screen
in the lenses.

"What are these for?" I asked still
feeling deflated in the moment.

"These will activate your hologram, and
you will be able to remotely direct your
hologram inside the library from out here
using your eye wear."

"But I . . ."

"Look, this is the only way for you to
get into the library without your DNA being
discovered in a maximum security building
you don't belong in. We don't want bells and
whistles going off or you getting caught.
So, follow my lead here. I know what I'm
doing." Jealousy of Dr. Muse's sense of
privilege sat heavy on my chest making it
hard to breath.

There was no use in arguing with her.
At this point I trusted her whole-heartedly
because she was being so protective of me.
If she wanted to turn me into the powers
that be, she would have done that back in

the Temple. With this thought of assurance, I crossed the transport area, glided to the playground and sat on one of the levitating pollywog pads the kids like to jump on. The disk made a sound like a wind-chime when I put my weight on it. I glimpsed back over my shoulder just long enough to see Rebekah's head descending into the round shoot with the blue, U.S. stamped, metal lid clanking shut behind her.

....

It seems I've had a lot of uninterrupted time to share my story with you lately. The time here is quite late. I must get some rest. I promise I'll relay more information to you soon. . .

....

It has been several weeks since I have had the ability to access my typewriter. I hope you haven't given up on me. Let me see. . .where was I . . .
Rebekah told me sliding through the mail-hole felt like it went on forever. However, she knew she was near the end of the shoot when the cylinder grew bigger into an expanse where the light at her feet looked like it was touching the very surface of a full moon. She was spit out like Jonah projected from the whale, and landed in a heap on the hard surface of the floor. This feeling, of the floor beneath her, shook her back to the reality she was in dream-time because in Alcheringa, time moves more slowly creating a heaviness in the body.

31

Scooping herself up, Rebekah said she then took out her holotrol, and pushed the button to activate my hologram.

It was at this point I stopped paying attention to the kids on the playground. I centered all my energies to the present mission, concentrating on the tools she had given me.

"Hey are you there?" I heard her voice in my ear.

"Yes, I hear you loud and clear. I can see every detail through the virtual glasses you gave me! I feel like I'm actually there!"

"You practically are; just in hologram form. Remember you have complete control. Just play it cool, and I'll get you to Thusia's works."

I could see the room was sterile, white, thin, and very elongated making Rebekah's transport down a long white marble corridor ominous. The further she transported, the more the walls seemed to part like the red sea. It widened into a spacious room that slowly grew. I looked around and was startled by its emptiness. For an archive, I wondered, *Where was all the physical material?*

"I know this being a new environment your mind must be reeling, but right about now I need you to concentrate on the task at hand for us to pull this off." Rebekah said this with urgency in her voice.

Being snapped back to my holographic environment, I turned on all my senses in the moment. I realized the rate of Rebekah's echoing footsteps had slowed. I didn't see it at first, but an object that blended in with the stark white walls started to come into view. Made of alabaster and marble, a stoic desk resonated a regimented governmental feel. Behind it sat an incongruent character. I noticed this stranger wearing a feminine white blouse. She, wearing a grey-haired wig, held her head bent low. I was barely able to capture the rim of her glasses. I kept seeing a movement of her arm repeating an up down motion that produced a kind of thumping sound that bounced down the corridor. As Rebekah and I (my hologram self) approached, I noticed a look of familiarity and recognition spread across Dr. Muse's face.

"Ze! Long time no see!" Rebekah said relaxed as a hot Louisiana afternoon.

The thumping sound suddenly stopped. Mahlah Zebach put down "his" government stamp that graced the front of tall stacks of papers almost hiding Zebach's face. My mind came into focus, and I realized that Mahlah was a male dressed in women's garb.

His appearance was quite disturbing. Mixed, matched clothing created a feast for the eyes keeping the mind guessing whether this person was truly male or female. It was not the elements of mixing a man's suit jacket with a flouncy white blouse or the young taste in jewelry contrasting the grey granny wig that bothered me. It was more her physique's appearance and skittish behavior. At a closer look, I guessed that Ze had been 'relived' several times (meaning in our culture, that your life has been sustained over several centuries due to medical advances). His skin appeared leathery and wrinkled. It was strange to see how emaciated he looked. I was very ill at ease sensing his nervous energy.

"Dr. Muse. . ." he said in a deep Louisiana accent, "I'm relieved that it is you coming down the hall of mirrors." He took a long drag of what looked like an e-cigarette, and exhaled smoke that changed different iridescent colors that almost glowed. I realized why I had not noticed the details of his appearance up to this point. At the same time, I hoped the smoke in the air would not reveal that I was trying to enter a security area as a hologram. At his mention of mirrors, I wondered why I hadn't noticed them when coming down the long hallway on our approach to the desk.

His demeanor seemed to change to a servant-obedience mentality with his interaction with Rebekah.

"I am at your service. Who do we have here?" Ze inquired, finally giving attention in my direction.

"Let me introduce you to T.R., my newest intern. I know you are used to my visits every year to introduce the interns to the old Earth remnants. It's quite a treat for them, especially since they are so young and don't have any memory of the old Earth. It's quite special to see the archeological artifacts and experience them first hand, don't you think?"

Ze confirmed his respect for Rebekah, "Why Yes Dr. Muse, I don't know what I would do if I didn't see your smiling face gracing the likes of the Science Archeological

Library. Our generation has much to thank you for, especially in your contributions to our very survival during the transition period. Being the keeper of the remnants, I agree they are worth protecting and worth remembering. Without remembering the past, we don't realize how privileged we are in our day and age."

Dr. Muse focused on her brilliance from the past and with an air of arrogance remarked, "I know there are many archives to consider. However, the transcripts we are interested in today are the writing remnants, specifically those of Thusia. T.R. doesn't really know what writing looks like, and has always been curious. T.R. has put to memory much of Thusia's work passed down through T.R.'s education. To see her original manuscripts would be especially meaningful."

"I would be happy to help you. Give me one moment to look up the artifacts' location."

I was quite surprised when Ze didn't question or banter me for more information, at least to make sure I was who I said I was. His lack of perusing me spoke volumes of Rebekah's authority in the situation.

Placing a shaky hand to the right corner of his glasses, Zebach's eyes scanned his lenses for the file's exact location. "Oh yes, you need to go back to the seventh mirror on the right, and you will find what you are looking for. . . and . . ." as he wrote on a piece of paper, "You'll need this. Here is the file access code."

Dr. Muse reached out to shake hands

with appreciation. Unexpectedly she took Mahlah Zebach's hand in hers, and drew it close. Lowering her face, she bent down to kiss it. On her face was a sarcastic grin that made the hairs on the back of my neck stand up. The awkward moment signaled that something deeper had happened to them both in their past. It was like observing a beautiful melody being sung with the accompanist playing the wrong supporting chords underneath.

Rebekah and I turned and retraced our transport down the long hallway. I now noticed the mirrors I swear were not there before. Each was unique and ornate with majestic frames embracing enchanted reflections on the walls.

"This is number seven. Now, what?" I asked inquisitively.

"Now, what seems hidden reveals the truth!" She said like a true scientist.

Dr. Muse began to read what was on the paper almost as if reading a spell. I took a quick glimpse into the mirror, and my heart sank when I noticed I did not have a reflection. A strange force I could feel took hold, and began to warp our appearance, literally sucking both of us into the power of the mirror's grasp.

I didn't realize how disorienting, difficult, and uncomfortable the truth might really be.

THE TRUTH SHALL SET YOU FREE

"People don't want to hear the truth because
they don't want their illusions destroyed."
-Frederick Nietzsche

"Why do my feet feel so heavy?" I asked
not recognizing my own voice. My words
sounded drawn out, an octave or two lower
than normal, and resembled the voice of
Satan. "Rebekah, what is happening?"
  "Well?" She said in a similar voice to
mine.
  I couldn't help but try out my new
sound by laughing in my most ghoulish,
satanic tone, "Ha, Ha, Ha!"
  "O.K. You are having too much fun with
this. Two can play at that game!"
  She hesitated a moment hiding a giggle
beneath her intention. "I'm coming for you!"
Rebekah sounding like a cross between a
drunk grizzly bear and a character from a
"B" rated horror flick, tried out her
monstrous voice.
  "Getting back to all seriousness, what
is happening to us?"
  It took so much time and effort to say
anything. Rebekah signaled to communicate
through our computerized eye-wear. Her first
message came across my screen.
  *Remember, we are in dream-time. What I
did not tell you is that dream-time slows
everything down: our voices, our movements,
even time itself.*
  *How does this affect us once we leave
the archive?* I asked trying to understand
the distortion of the environment.

She messaged back on my screen: *It means that when we leave with Thusia's work, time for us is moving slower thus taking us backward in time. It also means that for our present world these works don't exist, and won't be recognized as even being missing!*

I was in a state of confusion, and not technically understanding how all of this was happening. She assured me all of this was real, so I just went with it!

....

The Archive appeared as a wide-open space illuminated with bright light. In every direction around me I saw hundreds of clear orbs resembling crystal balls hanging in mid-air. I drew in a breath from the sheer beauty of the scene. Orbs of different sizes caught the brilliance of the light in such a way to create richly colored rainbows.

The scene brought back the ancient story of God's sign of the rainbow given as a promise not to destroy the whole Earth. It was a picture juxtaposed against the reality and irony of humanity's choice in my lifetime to destroy the whole Earth, the first Earth. Perhaps the rainbows all around me were reminding me of the promise of the revelation to come from Thusia's manuscripts. I wanted to understand more about why her writings were so threatening to the Mashiach.

Although I trusted Rebekah up to this point, observing the way she kissed Zebach's hand made me uneasy. Usually, I would just ignore my gut instinct convincing myself I was just reading into the gesture something that was not there. I was willing to give Rebekah the benefit of the doubt, and decided to sweep it under the rug.

Come closer. Over here, look! Rebekah drew me over to one of the orbs. They were breathtaking! Inside each one, on closer inspection, was a very well preserved specimen of written manuscript. Rebekah explained to me that each orb was a micro-environment that created the perfect preservation system regulating temperature, lighting, and clean-room conditions for each unique piece. The shape of the orb was intentionally crafted to magnify the writing so it could be read easily. The trick now was to find specifically what I was looking for.

In the middle of the room I saw an empty pedestal. At first I thought it looked out of place.

Rebekah, what is this? I messaged with my hands tempted to reach out and touch it.

That is known as the Precipice. An orb is placed on the Precipice to be read. Because of this tradition, the Precipice has become known as the seat of all knowledge. It is used as a tool to reference what you are looking for. Just concentrate. Stare at the top of the Precipice, and repeat in your mind, Thusia! Thusia! The energy from your mind will attract those orbs that you think of to come to where you are standing.

As I started the process the orbs began to vibrate. Putting more effort into my intent, I opened my eyes to see three orbs had responded to my beckoning, and hovered near me.

Can I touch them? I asked Rebekah, not knowing if they were security-alarmed in some way I was not aware of.

Most certainly, we have full access here.

I remotely commanded my hologram to reach out, and take the orb that hovered to my right. I was surprised that the orb was not hard in texture like smooth glass. Instead, it had more of a gel-like feel to it; very cool to the touch. I placed the orb carefully on the Precipice, and began to read.

Yes, this is one of Thusia's early works. I recognize it because I have read it before. This is when she was predicting that big business would become more powerful than the government and take over. A lot of people did not believe her or were so disillusioned with the government, they hoped she was right.

Rebekah was surprisingly silent, and did not respond to my computer message. I looked over to see her gesturing me to look at the next one. She pretended to run in slow motion towards the orb to make me laugh. *In dream-time, it would take me too long to bring it to you.* Her words came across my screen and then I heard a deep throated, "Ha! Ha!"

The second orb contained only a remnant of Thusia's later works. These were her most famous because her earlier predictions had come true. By that time, people took her more seriously. So much so that she had to go into hiding not to be prosecuted by the higher powers. They were very much against her making the truth known to the common people.

"Nothing here I'm not already familiar with." I said to Rebekah feeling discouraged.

"Try the third orb." Rebekah said walking around the room not really paying any attention to me.

Looking closer, I reached up to grab the orb in my hands. I got a cold chill up my spine from this little beauty. I knew in my deepest consciousness, I had found what I was looking for. The transcript was a long lost forgotten gem. There was a good chance it was a never known work by Thusia that at first glance seemed to be written during the Tribulation period. How did I know this? Because as a fellow writer I recognized, as in other historical accounts during times of persecution, writers will write in secret code. The symbols were extremely archaic. My heart leapt. However, I did not want to let on. Rebekah continued to wander about the room more fascinated with other writers' works in the archive.

"Find what you need?" She finally asked.

"Not quite. I'm still looking." I lied trying to conjure up a way to take this treasure back with me without Rebekah noticing. In that moment, I remembered I could set my eye gear on video mode.

Is it possible to hold the manuscript in my hands? This would mean so much to me in memory of Thusia. I stroked the orb longingly as if I was holding Thusia's very face in my hands.

Rebekah messaged back. *Sure, just poke the side of the orb with your finger.*

In an instant, the gel-like substance burst like a balloon, and the manuscript landed in my hands.

As I pretended to be reading it for the sake of Rebekah's presence I recorded the contents on my computer lens for later study. Back at my apartment, I could make an identical 3D model of Thusia's scroll from the information I recorded. I knew the importance of this discovery and did not want to share it with anyone, not even Rebekah. I knew its contents could be extremely important to understanding the truth as well as the future.

"Well?" Dr. Muse said in her 'devil' voice instead of messaging this time.

I messaged back. *This has been a wonderful almost spiritual experience. My seeing Thusia's work first hand has been enlightening. However, I have not found anything new here. I was hoping that there would be some revelation about where she had been all these years, how she was found, and why the Mashiach would sacrifice her in the Temple.*

A feeling of depression took over. I stared into space with tears welling up in my eyes thinking about her being gone forever. I privately thought to myself, *Thusia, your life was not in vain. I'll get to the bottom of this.*

Through the flood of emotion, I looked up, and saw Rebekah standing there with light shining all around her as if she were the fallen angel. With an eeriness in her voice, and a weird smile on her face, she snorted, "Come now, you don't want to do that. You don't want to end up like Thusia, do you?" My depression quickly melted into fear hearing Rebekah's unfamiliar tone, and reading the strange look in her eyes.

I felt the truth of the moment rush over me like a giant tidal wave. "Why did you bring me here?" I asked, frozen not knowing what to do.

"Well, if you stay in dream-time long enough, so much time will pass that you cannot find your way back to your own truth."

I could tell Rebekah's intentions on bringing me here were questionable. She was testing me to see how much she could control me. Bringing me here in hologram form was a way for her to find that out. Her relationship with me was for her agenda only. I felt as if someone had just slapped me across the face, poured ice water over my head, and shouted in a blood curdling scream. "Wake up!"

In my new awareness of Rebekah, I decided to run back towards the mirror that acted as our portal. Running, mind you, was in slow motion, almost impossible. I attempted to get out of the situation. I felt the circumstance very disingenuous on Rebekah's part. As I tried to make my escape, a sucking motion in the opposite direction picked my feet up off the floor and pulled me backwards. *What is happening?* Dread filled my mind.

We've stayed too long. Rebekah messaged. *Dream-time has reached its tipping point. Any movement towards getting back is futile. Now, why don't you give me what you really found in the archive.* Rebekah grabbed my leg and clawed at me like a desperate animal. I took my other foot, and kicked her head with as much force as I could muster. I felt her grasp let go. I looked back just enough to see her get sucked into the black vortex.

I slowly reached up to the rim of my glasses, pushed the atomize button, and gave the voice command. "Eject!"

I found myself breathing heavily as if I had just run a marathon. Beads of sweat fell from my brow. I could hear the thumping of my heartbeat from the realization of what just happened. My eyes popped open to see children playing all around me in gleeful tones. I was swept back into reality by the sound of chimes beneath me as I shifted my weight. I couldn't believe I was back on the pollywog pad on the playground. *I am alive! I cannot believe I survived!* I took a moment to take a deep breath. My mind continued, *Perhaps the same was not true for Rebekah!* The thought of her left a bad taste in my mouth.

....

NOTE TO READER: From this point on you need to consider if you want to take the risk to continue. It is one thing to risk my own life in the telling of this story. However, I do not intend to risk your life in the sharing of the knowledge that I am giving you. As this suggests, the chances of Rebekah still being alive and existing in the past is real. For all I know she could exist in *your* time period. Coming across these writings would put you in a predicament. This is not my intent to put you in a compromising position. If you feel your chances of coming across Rebekah are low or next to none, then I would encourage you to continue your journey with me so that you can act to help change the course of future events for humanity's benefit. Please continue to use discretion in who you share this information with. In the future Rebekah has her ways. In the past, I am sure this is equally true. My prayers are that my story does not land in the wrong hands, in my present day, or in yours.

THE VISIT

"Deep into the darkness peering, long I stood there, wondering, fearing, doubting, dreaming, dreams no mortal ever dared to dream before." -Edgar Allan Poe

Buzzz! The sound was annoying. *Buzzz!* I felt the flutter of pesky wings pass by my ear, and tiny hairy legs grip the tip of my nose. *BUZZZ!* The sound was louder, more intense. *Sllaappp!* My hand instinctively hit my face thinking that on its descent it was smashing a nagging bee. Shocked into reality, I realized in my sleep-state I mistook the sound of my alarm for an Anthophila. This was not the best way to start my day. I lay there like a lazy lump still feeling the effects of being in *Alcheringa,* dream-time.

The buzzing continued. I mustered up enough momentum to turn, pound my alarm clock into submission, and notice the date staring back at me: MAY.24.416. N.H.E.

I still could not believe it was true! My exposure to the Alcheringa Project at the archeological library had taken me back in time. When my consciousness returned to the playground yesterday, I didn't realize I existed in time, just two weeks earlier. My body seemed to fight to know how to recover its energy. Time travel is hard on the body. I guess one advantage is that I'm two weeks younger even though I don't feel like it. A knocking sound to my left redirected my thoughts, and I focused my senses towards the glass door.

Right on time. I thought. It was Anesi. Shuffling his little feet back and forth he maneuvered his spaceball. It kept banging into the little pet door he used to make his usual entrance. I aimed my remote in his direction releasing the mechanism while greeting him with "Entre vu!" The knocking stopped after Anesi entered the room. His spaceball spun past my bed as I observed his little legs running. He and I both knew the morning routine, and I looked forward to it every day. I grinned when I heard the attractive clink of magnetic parts kiss, indicating his spaceball had made contact with the hydro-tube. Next I heard white noise signaling me that the tiny hydraulic door was released for Anesi to enter the hydro-tube.

This eco-system extended up the wall, and filled my ceiling with what looked like a labyrinth. Its exit was an extended tube that hung down over my bed. The tubing resembled a piece of art with all its different colors and possibilities for decision making. My eyes followed the movements of my wonderful fuzzy chipmunk chipet who had been my companion since I had been in hiding.

I held my breath anticipating 'the drop.' To make it more fun, I closed my eyes. Suddenly, I let out an embarrassing giggle as if I were eight years old again experiencing an amusement park ride. I felt his tiny furry feet land, tickle my belly, and scurry two laps from under my chin to the top of my head. He would only stop long enough to wiggle his whiskers in my ear. In response, I would scream with delight and break out in chills. On the second lap around my face, I heard his tiny whispers in my ear, "You are my world! My love is coming your way!" Anesi proceeded to run with great speed through my pajamas as if contemplating strategies of escape in a weird looking hydro-tube. It was a wonderful way to wake up in the world, forget my worries and be reminded I was not alone.

Our routine ended with my chipmunk chipet lying on his back, under my chin exhausted, and expecting belly rubs. Using one finger to stroke his soft fur, I hummed a little tune. The vibrations of my voice made my little companion relax, if just for a moment.

....

Although I was still exhausted, I decided to turn on my holovision to catch the morning news. The difference between holovision and television is that no matter where I am in my room, the picture faces me in three-dimensional form. I think you would really like it.

Watching my holovision from my bed caused me to continue to drift in and out of sleep. My ears and mind were awake, but I could not keep my eyes open. The newscaster's voice was so soothing that in my half dream-state I imagined at times Thusia was alive and talking to me. My ears zoomed in, more intent on the announcer's words at the mere mention of the date "June 6th."

News anchor Carisse Nuvo continued,
"Today in world news. . It has been
reported by High Counselor Modsiw that the
Mashiach will be making pilgrimage to the
Temple mount on June 6th in celebration of
the High Priestess' birthday. This is an
unprece-dented appearance by her highness.
There is a feeling of anticipation, and much
excitement in the air. To get a glimpse of
one of the most powerful figures of our time
is a rarity. The Temple plaza is expected to
be overflowing with one million people in
attendance."

June 6th, I kept repeating to myself.
The words finally made their way to being
audible, "June 6th!"

"Anesi, do you know what this means?"

"Whoohoo!" I started jumping up and
down on my bed like a kid.

"Anesi, this means today is May 24th.
June 6th has not happened yet. Thusia is
still alive!! I have a chance to save her. I
cannot believe it!"

I flopped on the bed, and turned up the
volume. At that moment, there was an
interference with my holovision. It fizzed
in and out with other random images
interrupting the news report. I looked
closer, and my eyes grew bigger, as I
watched the reporter's lips moving speaking
gibberish. Carisse Nuvo's head began to do a
slow three hundred and sixty degree turn.
When her face made its way back to a forward
position, my mouth dropped open. It was the
face of Ze!

"Hello T.R. Do not be afraid. I come to
you in peace."

My heart started to race like a toy that was wound too tight and suddenly let go. I thought, *how did Ze find me here? If he knows I'm here, who else knows?* I started to panic.

Ze continued, "Again, I tell you, do not be afraid." His hand extended out from the holovision laying his palm on my forehead, and with his touch all fear left my body. "I come with wisdom on your behalf. My words are meant to encourage and strengthen you. What you need to know is IN the code. Have faith in my guidance for you. Be assured, you have everything needed within you. My added wisdom and guidance will guarantee your success and your survival!" I sensed in my soul that Ze had the ability to know the future. In the holovision, Ze looked at me with a wry smile, stood up from behind the news desk, and with a wink in my direction began to walk away.

Suddenly, a need welled up to the surface of my being to yell out to him. In that moment, I shouted, "Ze!" My body sat straight up in the bed with so much force my chipet went flying! The only sound in the room was Carisse Nuvo giving the weekly forecast by waving her wand. This created three-dimensional weather effects that were hard to go unnoticed.

Ignoring the entertainment value, I used my remote to turn the holovision off and back on again. My thoughts tried to catch up with what had just happened. I must have dreamt the whole encounter! I resolved, *Ze, is right! I feel more determined now than ever to figure out Thusia's code because her voice and her vision deserve to be heard. Today is the day!*

THE CIPHER

"The art of simplicity is a puzzle of
complexity."
-Douglas Horton

It is getting more dangerous for me to
come to you and type these entries. It is
most imperative I pass this information on
to you. I know it is my destiny and my
calling to do so. Sometimes, I feel that
your receiving of my message is our only
hope. There is an urgency to relay to you my
discoveries revealed through Thusia's coded
manuscript. I find it ironic yet empowering
that you live before the time of the new
Heaven and Earth, and I live in it. My
ability to communicate with you gives me
hope in my darkest time. I fear that I will
be snuffed out before revealing the
information that is so important. Perhaps
humanity will have another chance to get it
right! You may be thinking *Why me? Why am I
chosen for this pivotal work?* I ask myself
the same question all the time. Just know
you are not alone. There is someone in the
universe, who understands. . .

....

I had taken the time to make an exact
duplicate of the scroll with my 3D machine.
Technology made it possible for me to
recreate its exact likeness using original
materials to experience the authenticity of
interacting with the document as much as

possible. I looked around my eco-pod to find a place to study Thusia's work. My floating desk would be perfect if only I didn't have so much clutter! I picked up my tea cup magnetized to the desk top, and used my other hand to swish everything off my desk only for my possessions to float freely in the air around me as if I lived in a space junkyard. I didn't care. The excitement of being a detective, figuring out Thusia's tantalizing puzzle was all I had on my mind. I was all in for the long haul.

Since I was barefoot, I had to push against furniture to propel myself back to my bed. Holding on with both hands to the bottom edge of the frame, my feet floated up. I looked like I was doing a hand stand. I bent my elbows to look deep under the shadowed underbelly. I reached to the center of the cradle that held my prized possession, and carefully untied the leather binding that held it there. When it lightly floated into my grasp I could not help but think how that moment contrasted the heaviness of its secret contents. I had a sense of heightened responsibility realizing I was the caregiver of such a priceless object. I wondered, what will it reveal?

I was reminded of Thusia's reading in the Temple. "May the generations who fought for freedoms of expression before me, and those who continue the fight after me, prevail above all powers that be to suppress them." Her words refreshed my courage to find out the truth, and to do something about it. When she said, "the Word is flesh" I was reminded that the written word is a

53

living word because it calls us to action
for change. This is what Thusia was
communicating through this scroll that I
found. By writing it in code, she was
letting me know how crucial the information
was, and that my search would not leave me
empty handed.

I carefully made my way to the table.
Before I unrolled the scroll, I made sure to
put on a pair of spray-on gloves. The scroll
was over five hundred years old and needed
protecting. Unrolling the precious cargo, I
was amazed by how well preserved the
document was. The texture of the material
felt more like animal skin than any type of
parchment. The two decorative poles that
held the scroll were made of bronze and cast
in the shapes of planets and constellations.
The intricacy of the symbols proved her
writing was very labor intensive. I observed
the intentionality and precision in each
handmade symbol. The very detailed shapes at
first glance gave the appearance of a
repeated pattern in the code writing. The
elaborate swirling curves of the ink
appeared so ornate that the document could
be mistaken for a work of art. Perhaps this
is the reason no one really paid much
attention to it.

The way the figures were spaced on the
material was the first clue that told me I
was looking at an idiosyncratic object.
Since all the figures looked identical, I
searched other ways the code might be
different. I looked at color variations,
possible size differences, even turning the
script upside down. Scanning it, I made sure

it wasn't a hologram. (Although I knew it wouldn't be one because holograms didn't exist during the time of the great Tribulation). This test helped me authenticate that the scroll was truly as old as I thought it was.

Perhaps what I was looking for was smaller than the human eye could see. Yes! My microscope, why hadn't I thought of it before? I was excited at the thought of inspecting Thusia's manuscript so intimately. The privilege helped me feel close to her again.

I must have looked in every nook and cranny. I searched everywhere I had remembered using my microscope. Where in the hell can it be? I hurled my dirty laundry up into the air then rushed over to the dish washer, and looked inside. I know that sounds crazy, but I was desperately looking for all the possibilities. Feeling out of breath, frustrated, and adrenaline drained, I flopped and floated lotus style with a dirty pair of exercise pants deciding to land, and hug my head. With the thought of giving up, I blew the pant strings that were tickling my nose.

No! I'm not giving up! The voice of reason came back to me.

All I need is a way to clear my head. I just need to take some time to step away, regroup, and rest my mind. Then it will come to me. I decided to put into practice what I always do when I am tense, under pressure, and need a clear way to problem solve.

This is a time for. . .the Ziggurat! The Ziggurat was my retreat, my oasis,

almost my religion. Well, I can at least say
I've had religious experiences in that
space. It was my favorite place to just be
me. This was my self-made sanctuary. I'm so
glad I decided to build one into my ecopod.

A Ziggurat was traditionally a stacked
pyramid built by the Chaldeans to reach
higher in the sky to observe the cosmos.
This fulfilled their love of astronomy and
astrology. Since our ecopods already exist
in the sky (some of us live higher than
others), I thought it would be a cool idea
to build a Ziggurat into my roof. It's a
quiet private space I can go to observe
celestial beings on my own terms. A rung-
less ladder gives me a way to propel myself
upwards through a small passage way that
opens into a beautifully constructed
pressure glass encasement where I can see in
all directions. I have a panel that opens to
the outdoors allowing the lens of my
telescope to extend even closer to the
stars. I sit comfortably on a levitating
ecto-sphere that moves with my shifting
weight, and turns in any direction. I take a
lot of pride in creating a space for my own
enjoyment; my own sanity for that matter. If
ever I needed it, I need it now.

The stars were like liquid silver
suspended on onyx, teasing me with their
twinkling winks. If only I could reach out
and grab one. Thusia was even more beautiful
than this sight. My mind surged with the
thought of saving her. I wondered if the
decoding would reveal information to help me
on my quest. I felt like I was in dreamland
as I looked through my telescope, in awe of

the nine moons. Each one had its own
distinct characteristics; all habitable,
mind you. I guess I haven't mentioned them
to you up to now. I will tell you more about
them later. They are worth explaining to
you. The night continued to draw me in, and
remind me just how incredible the universe
truly is.

After relaxing in the Ziggurat for a
couple of hours, a clanking and thumping
sound from below made me look down between
my legs. The perspective was the same as
looking through a telescope.

"Anesi, what sort of sorcery are you up
to?" He zipped with his H-pack below me
where I could see him.

"I am magic!" He said not explaining
but giving a tiny smile along with a giggle.

He chimed in at me, "Time to come
down!" He pointed and curled his tiny finger
back and forth beckoning me to come to where
he was. He then zoomed out of my sight
range.

I edged off my ecto-sphere, raised my
arms above my head, and floated downward. As
I searched for Anesi, my eyes landed on his
fuzzy body, relaxed leaning against my
microscope now sitting on my floating table.
Did I mention he was eating that puffy
cheese snack treat that you might know of?
(Yes, they still exist only they are purple
now).

"Anesi, where in the world did you find
it?"
Anesi just wiped his knuckles across his
chest, and then blew on them like a 'cool
dude.' "Next time, you might think of asking

me or getting me to help when you are in such a fickle pickle."

I was so excited about the prospect of getting started on the project. I didn't inquire any further. All I could think to do was lean over, take a bite from Anesi's purple puffy snack, and kiss him between his tiny ears.

"Thank you, buddy." His whiskers snickered as I gave him another salty treat.

Pinching his H-pack between two fingers, I lifted Anesi. Then I let go leaving him drifting in mid-air happily snacking. It was time for me to get down to business. I was determined to stay up all night if that is what it would take to break the code.

I thought as I placed my eye against the microscope lens that I was about to discover a whole new world like looking through a telescope that gives more clarity. I felt so close to deciphering the code. I thought I could hear it speaking to me. Perhaps I was the first person the manuscript was talking to since Thusia's writing of it. What would it say?

On closer inspection, the microscope revealed one tiny detail not seen by the naked eye. On each symbol, a movable notch shaped like an arrowhead presented itself in different positions. After full analysis, I determined the whole cipher was made up of only eight carefully placed arrowheads on a repeated symbol pattern. At this point I knew they didn't represent letters. More than likely, they represented numbers. What kind of numbers? Computer code? Longitude?

Latitude? Important bank numbers? The possibilities were endless. The last thing I remember is the taste of tea leaves on my tongue, the whizzing sound of a flying chipet, seeing the crack of dawn on my head's way down; the meeting of a mind, a desk, and sleep.

....

I had the sensation of swinging back and forth, back and forth in wide sweeps at a high altitude. I felt the coolness on my body with the rocking motion. My arms reached strangely above my head suspended somehow. . . at first out of focus now becoming clear I was confused about where I was. The sound of circus music set the scene. "Whoooo!!" I looked down as the circus tent seemed to sway to and fro. *How did I get up here? How is it I'm in the middle of an acrobat routine?* My mind in survival mode finally turned its attention to the figure hanging upside down on a swing holding tightly to my uplifted arms. I looked up.

"Well. . . hello again, my friend. . .fancy finding you here!"

"Ze, what in hell is going on? What are you doing here?"

"I'm here to show you something!" And with that, on the last swing out, he threw me with all his might and let go. I swiftly flew grabbing at the atmosphere yelling like a little girl.

Next, all I knew was my mouth was full

of sand and I was surrounded by desert. My body was deposited, prostrate at the bottom of an ancient Ziggurat. I stood up, brushed off my pride, and began to ascend the dozens of steps. Each one represented a day in the calendar. My circumstance was my life's dream. I always wanted to experience an authentic Ziggurat. The timing of my ascent was perfect. As the sun was setting it cast beautiful shadows that danced with shades of purple and pink on polished stone. When I reached the landing at the top of the staircase I noticed a small opening where I could enter the tallest point on this sacred structure. I took a deep breath and walked in. The strong smell of smoky incense filled the space, and I hesitated when I saw a dark figure standing on the other side of the room. The stranger was peering through the astronomical observance tools used in the age of the Chaldeans.

"Who are you?" I asked with my spirit in tune to the moment. The dark robed entity slowly turned to reveal its face. I was frozen. I couldn't move.

"I thought you would never ask. I am your spirit guide. I have been with you all along, protecting you, and watching over you." I collapsed on the floor in disbelief fighting back tears knowing all this time I had not been alone or without a higher purpose! The familiar figure came closer bent down, gently placed a hand under my chin raising my unbelieving eyes.

"Ze, I can't believe it's you! Why are we here?"

"Come take my hand. I have something to

show you." And with Ze's tender hand in mine, he led me to a window that opened to the stars.

"Look out there. Tell me what you see."

"I see, what you see Ze. The stars, planets, a whole universe bigger than us is out there!"

Ze continued, "I'm trying to help you. Let me put it this way, what did the Chaldeans see?"

"Why, I don't know what you are trying to say Ze."

"I'm trying to help you. . .I'm trying to help you. . ." His words started to drift off.

I felt a tiny figure yanking my earlobe, and saying directly into my ear. "I'm trying to help you, now wake up and get back to work. You are drooling all over Thusia's scroll."

I had fallen asleep only to be woken up by Anesi whispering sweet nothings in my ear. The dream was so prolific and vivid it felt so real. What was Ze trying to tell me? I tried to put it together. *The Ziggurat. . .looking at the stars. . .the Chaldeans.* I stopped.

"Eureka!" I exclaimed and my heart skipped a beat.

What system uses eight numbers? The ancient Chaldean numerology chart! Ze you are a genius! Now I had what I needed to decipher the code.

....

It has taken me a full week to

translate Thusia's prophesies that she coded
before the time of Armageddon. Its value is
pertinent for me to share with you. I will
send the transcriptions to you in three
different letters. All three are of great
significance to my current plea for help.
The contents of the cipher include: the
signs, the wonders, and the revelations. In
my current state of remaining in hiding it
is even more urgent that I get these letters
to you. Be on the lookout . . .

LETTER #1: THE SIGNS

"The world as we have created it is a process of our thinking. It cannot be changed without changing our thinking."
-Albert Einstein

Remember, Thusia's prophesies were written in the Tribulation period before Armageddon in 2100 A.C.E. It is now 416 N.H.E. I cannot tell you how accurate, I mean scary accurate her predictions are. Her warning begins:

"I see a future time when all seems at peace, but at what cost? Secretly, those who write the written word, known as the 'word in flesh', will be banned and killed. Only memory is allowed in society because it demonstrates the power of the human mind. Peace is only a farce. . . a way to control."

There is so much back story that I need to give you so that you will understand how much credence there is to what Thusia is saying. I know because I am living it now and I've seen the progression of the signs that have come to pass. Everything has proven to be true. If only I knew of Thusia's manuscript in the beginning, before Armageddon. Perhaps I could have made a difference in the legacy of history. All I can hope is that I am doing so now in sharing this with you.

....

Thusia's warnings proclaim four signs to look for. I knew something was coming in the changes I saw, but I did not realize the magnitude at the time. I would say the beginnings could be seen in the early 2090's A.C.E. The early signs were in my first life, before I was relived. People were getting fed up with the government. Most of the population didn't realize that a lot of their opinions were being swayed and wooed by advertisements that spoon-fed and brainwashed their thinking. Television was a huge research project conducted on the general populous without their permission. What I am telling you is ironic. Do you know who was behind the research that produced the results of these studies? You got it. . .the government! You might be thinking *Why would the government use their ability to coerce the public to convince the people to turn against the governing bodies?* This is where it gets interesting. Per Thusia's prediction, big business would take over, and government control would wane.

I saw this first sign come to fruition back in 2085 A.C.E. when the government provided funding to Dr. Mahlah Zeback, a government employed neuroscientist. At the time, he was provided government funding to head up the human brain study and human genome project. He was highly renowned for his contributions awarded the Nobel Prize for his research. Then, there was a slow turning. Government influences began to decrease, and large business gained more power. All the work that Dr. Zebach had done was sold to the corporate world, and what did they do? They used it to sway the people's way of thinking about the government. The resulting affect? Dr. Zeback was asked to step down from his position, stripped of his Nobel Prize, and forced into menial labor.

The section of Thusia's code that brings up Dr. Zebach explains so much to me in my first meeting with him at the library. I understand why he appeared to me to be so nervous at the time. But there is more to Ze than meets the eye. You and I are both aware of Ze's true role, but Thusia is not. She does not know that Ze is my spiritual guide, and has been even way back then. It's hard for me to wrap my mind around that thought.

What specific businesses were involved in taking over to be more powerful than the government, you may be asking? What sign does Thusia warn to look for that signals the beginnings of this taking place? Believe it or not, one of the first places this began was through job applications, government surveys, and census; the simple checking of the box. She goes on to say, when you start to notice a change in regulations that requires a gathering of different kinds of information, this is a true sign of major events to come. In society, back in the early 2090's, it became illegal to ask about race, gender or economic status. So, people became categorized by T.Y.P.E.s. These T.Y.P.E.s were secretly set up by big business to keep tabs on how much the human population was using their products or influenced by their services. On the census, survey or job

application people would check which
T.Y.P.E. they were per what services they
used and how often. Thusia reveals in the
cipher that the acronym T.Y.P.E. stands for:
The T.aking of Y.our P.ersonal E.volution.

In the beginning this included a "G"
T.Y.P.E meaning government services, but
this was slowly phased out. At the time, the
public saw this as a positive change
expressed by popular opinion because less
government control meant more power to the
people, right? Wrong!

Thusia then reveals the "P" T.Y.P.E.
This represented pharmaceuticals. She says
to watch for the influence of advertisements
that make the population feel like they must
rely on medications to keep them healthy.
This is the beginnings of mind control of
the masses. The "Pharm's" influence would be
reinforced through the entertainment indus-
try; the best example being television. They
rely on these methods to dumb down the human
mind from having to think on its own. My
personal observations and per research
statistics that I have found by the year
2100 A.C.E., 95% of the world's population
was purchasing prescription drugs. That
meant within a ten-year period, almost
everyone living was a "P" T.Y.P.E.

There were also "S" T.Y.P.E.s that had
just as much of an influence on the world's
population. "S" T.Y.P.E.s started earlier in
history during the industrial revolution and
the coming of age of science. The pharmaceutical companies came into power but not
alone. The scientific community was holding
the hand of the pharmaceutical companies; a

marriage of sorts. Thusia warns there will
be a time of accelerated scientific advance-
ment that will thrill the masses. Technology
will mesmerize the minds of the people and
will open an opportunity for the taking of
liberties and freedoms. The people will
support technology and willingly participate
as "S" T.Y.P.E.s. The danger, Thusia warns,
is that science will come in the name of
good. The reality though is the scientific
community will use those advance-ments to
gain control over the populous.

The last category that Thusia reveals
is the hardest for me to talk about because
I personally survived it. Like Thusia, I
experienced the time of the Tribulation and
am a survivor of Armageddon.

By the year 2100 A.C.E. tensions had
mounted around the world concerning those
who were "R" T.Y.P.E.s. Those individuals
in this category were the religious ones who
argued over their beliefs concerning "The
Word." Factions and disunity in the beginning only caused small pockets of religious
groups to become terrorists. But because of
the relentless passion of religious fanati-
cism, they could sway the influences of the
"P" and "S" T.Y.P.E.s who were now in
control. The world was set up for the beginnings of a revolution. People's varied
interpretations of "The Word" (meaning any
sacred text), and how it was lived out in
the world, created friction among a variety
of different sects.

Many people did not see this as one of
the signs of the coming of Armageddon
because they were too busy looking for the

signs spelled out in the book of Revelations
such as the rebuilding of the Temple. Thusia
explains that this served as a deterrent to
the real signs; a kind of red herring. She
warns in her prophesy not get stuck in the
details, and instructs those who will listen
to look to the bigger picture of events.

When the warning signs of the waning of
government, the coming of power of big
business, the numbing of the human mind
through scientific and medicinal means, and
religious unrest worldwide become cultural
reality, these are the prequel, tell-tale
signs to look for in the setting up of
Armageddon.

....

I cannot believe how many insights
Thusia's writings have provided. I have
lived through a lot of what she talks about.
I had to sit down when she revealed Dr.
Rebekah Muse's active participation during
the Tribulation period. I was shocked by
what I found out.

In the same time frame, in the 2090's,
Dr. Muse was serving as a Biolonic Pharma-
Medical Engineer for a prestigious company.
I found out at the time she partnered with
Dr. Mahlah Zebach, and they worked together
for a time. Mahlah's research from the
human brain study was combined with
developments from the genome project. His
results were used to support Dr. Muse's work
on how to prolong life. This was one of
Rebekah's passions. She was a master mind in
understanding the complex systems of the

human body, computers, and pharmacology. The reason I trusted Dr. Muse in my encounter with her is because she was known for her humanitarian efforts.

During the years of Armageddon, even during the time of transition in the years following, Rebekah's first development was the one she used on me back in her lab. As you know, she developed medicinal food patches that sustained people after the largest war in history. When people couldn't access basic human resources for survival, she was the savior who provided a life-giving food source.

Her second contribution to mankind, shortly after the creation of the new Heaven and new Earth, was her breakthrough on how to extend human life. Now, people had the choice for the first time to "relive" if they wanted to. I personally have "relived" four times, which makes me four hundred and sixty-six years old. I know this may come as a shock to you, but in the future, this is common place. Because Dr. Muse was so prestigious and praised for her contri-butions, I was extremely surprised by what Thusia revealed next.

Thusia's prophesies warn against Dr. Muses' work because she appears as someone she is not. In the new Heaven and the new Earth, she will use both her medicinal food and ability to "relive" to take power for her alone and manipulate a "zombie" nation. Thusia even states that this 'influence' will be found in the Temple keeping the Mashiach close to her. I put two and two together, and figured out she was talking about Rebekah.

....

You are my only hope! If you begin to see any of these signs, take heed! Be forwarned against those who come as wolves in sheep's clothing claiming they come to help make humanity better. They have a secret agenda that leads to the destruction of the first Earth. Believe me, when someone like me has been through the worst war in history, anything looks better. Most people would be willing to do anything to survive. Humanity, like Noah, will look to the second Earth to be their 'garden of Eden' when, in fact they will be taking 'a bite of the fruit' without even knowing it.

Thusia's last warning:

Do not look to the sky or stars for signs and wonders

Do not look to "the Word" for signs and wonders

Do not look to Jerusalem for signs and wonders

Listen!
Watch and listen!
They are all around you!

Wake up!

LETTER #2: THE WONDERS

"One expected growth; change, without it,
the world was less, and the well of
inspiration dried up, the muses fled."
-Charles De Lint

I know that the amount of information I'm sharing may be overwhelming for you. I hope I haven't discouraged you or made you question the validity of what I am saying. I appeal to your compassion to understand my situation. What would you do in my position? I am hiding for my life only long enough to get my story out in hopes that history can be altered and not be repeated. I hope you are still there . . . still listening!

....

I promised I would share with you more about the nine moons. I am still trying to process the revelation around their true purpose that Thusia refers to. I can't believe it! Let me start at the beginning, and tell you what I know to be true before telling you the ciphered information of Thusia's code.

After the destruction and devastation of most of the world's governmental structures due to Armageddon, those who survived got together, and formed the World Union. The organization was made up of very educated people. It included some of the world's most renowned scientists. One of the most prestigious was the Professor of Research and Development at Manhattan Academy of Sciences. He wasn't just well

71

known for his research on planetary generation. He was most well known for being a descendent of Robert Oppenheimer, the creator of the atomic bomb. Because of his experience, and aptitude he was elected as the chief scientist at the Bureau of the New World Order. It is because of his work that the second Earth came into existence.

This explains the new Earth, but what about the new Heaven? Once humanity was established on the new Earth, rules of governing changed. Peace was on the forefront of the World Union's mind. All nations were asked to place in video form a treaty agreeing to keep peace even with those who were different from them in culture and beliefs. The second part of the treaty made any form of writing against the law. Those who chose to disobey would be put to death. Yes, you heard me correctly! This decree did not just apply to sacred texts anymore but all written materials. Because "The Word" was the cause of the third world war, the powers that be did not want history to repeat itself.

Maintaining peace and committing all things to memory was the cultural norm ingrained into society and was demanded by the New World Order. The treaty stated that all nations would come together to live in peace and diversity, to uphold liberty and equality for all peoples, and to celebrate differences. But there were nations that did not agree with the New World Order's decree. Because of this, a compromise was agreed upon.

A solution involved the genius of the

chief scientist who had discovered anti-
gravity, the one who had made the creation
of the new Earth possible. He decided to put
his discovery to the test on a larger scale.
He, along with a team of scientists,
discovered a way to "lasso" nine of the most
viable moons in our solar system, and bring
them into orbit around the new Earth. This
was a herculean feat and did not happen
overnight. Once the moons were in orbit,
they were in what was known as the
"Goldilocks Zone." Each one began to quickly
adapt, and the moons became habitable for
human life. Nations wishing to remain
autonomous by keeping their own cultural
identity could live separate from humanity
by taking up residence on the nine moons;
each bearing a name of one of the nine Muses
of Zeus. This is what the World Union told
the public and what I have known to be true
all my life. Thusia reveals a different
truth.

Per Thusia's manuscript, the nine moons
were not really used for uncooperative
nations. They were used to hold the private
elite with all their riches and amenities.
There was a cover up by the New World Order
to protect the powers that be, for those in
control to continue their influence and
manipulation without being found out by the
public. You might say, out of sight out of
mind. Instead of creating a true peaceful
paradise on the new Earth, an illusion was
being created instead. The goal was to
guarantee a drugged obedience of submission
of the public, ultimately taking away the
identity of the individual. By taking away

the written word, those in control took away one of the only places an individual could speak freely with resolve.

The time and energy that went into warping the ways of thinking of people into believing the written word was a curse to humanity. The main cause of the third world war was a set up by the elite. Planting this belief into the minds of the people, slowly over time, turned them away from thinking of the written word as being good. It turned them away from reflecting on the power of individual expression. The act of writing from this point on, in my world, the new Earth, meant a death sentence.

Per Thusia, the nine Muses serve the elite, and give them their own heavens to live in. Why would they do this, you may be asking? The cipher talks about the elite taking this action in case the people of new Earth revolt, and the Earth is destroyed again. This way the people would be annihilated, and a new Earth would not have to be created again. They would each have their own "Earth" to do with as they please. What I have observed in my current position is if the people are under the hypnotic state of those in control, the elite are happy to continue the status quo. Who do I have to thank for manipulating the system? Who is the grand master making all this possible? Why, the chief scientist of the New World Order; Ophis Phineus!

LETTER #3: THE REVELATIONS

"For all that is secret will eventually be brought into the open . . ."(NLT, Luke 8:17)

As I concentrated on the next section of the scroll, I continued a nervous habit I have had for many years. My finger resting lightly on its edge, rhythmically pressed, pushed, released-pressed, pushed, released until I heard a whirring sound of the hovering saucer holding my tea cup at my shoulder level. I could not resist the intertwining, complicated personality of fig and flower sitting on my tongue through tiny sips of tea leaves that eased the difficulty of un-deciphered code. Although what I had discovered so far was intriguing and eye-opening, my body felt seized with the notion that I was about to dig even deeper into a greater unknown. One that might change my whole way of thinking, my whole way of being.

I was snapped out of the moment by the sound of some kind of gibberish. The verbalizations were animalistic whatever they were. My curiosity drew my eyes to the corner of the room where Anesi, mesmerized in front of a tiny mirror, stood on hind legs, and held a walnut in one hand.

"Anesi, what are you doing?"

"Oh, I just wanted to see what it would be like to speak 'chipmunk' instead of human for once..."

"Well?" I said, wanting to know more.

"*Well* what?"

"Please translate. What were you saying

in 'chipmunk'?"

Holding the walnut high in the air, he got down on one knee and began.

"Chip-chi-cher-ch-chu . . .How do I love thee . . .Che-chee-chou-ch-cha . . .Let me count the ways."

Insert here the rolling of my eyes. I thought to myself, *This is how a chipet passes the time when it is bored?*

I proceeded in a half joking tone, "Anesi, remind me to reprogram you the first chance I get!" He stopped admiring his walnut, and gave me a look that anyone could read no matter what language they spoke. I gave a sigh, and got back to the business at hand.

I had reached a section in the scroll that seemed to have a slightly different pattern than the rest of the manuscript. I started to write with my finger in the air the numeric sequence. The numbers would then automatically appear on a holographic screen directly above my desk where I could perform my analysis at eye level. There were some advantages of having been with Rebekah Muse. My ability to successfully build my own hologram was one of them.

The numerology was indicating a list of names. I continued to play around with the letters and numbers as I began. The first name appeared- "David." I continued. After several hours, I had deciphered forty-one names, the first three read, "David-Nathan-Mattatha." The last three in the sequence read, "Heli-Joseph-Jesus." Thusia had included the genealogy of Jesus, taking the bloodline back to King David much like in

the gospel of Luke. Her prophesy continued,
*The first coming of Christ is in the
form of a male . . .*

Why would Thusia include this
information from the past that is already
known? She must be setting the stage for
what is coming next in her revelation. Now
I was even more interested in the portion of
the scroll I had not translated yet. This
was just whetting my appetite.

At the exact moment of thinking those
words, my stomach let out a grumbling noise.
I decided to satisfy my ravishing hunger
with some of my favorite Zezuble. Studying
so hard, I often forget to eat. During each
delicious mouthful, I anticipated the
importance of the revelations of Thusia, and
braced myself for what I would find out
next.

I continued to work passionately
through the night with each ciphered symbol
satisfying a craving inside me like a child
savoring each sticky lick of a lollipop.
Every bite of information I took in, and
digested; tasting morsels of Thusia's
predictions. I could not believe what I was
reading:

*"The first coming of the Christ in the form
of a male
The second coming of the Messiah in the form
of a female
From the royal bloodline- of Jesus
You will know this person as the "Oben"
She will be foreshadowed by false prophets
But will be hidden no longer*

*Her true identity will be revealed to all
the world
This will fulfill the salvation
God intended . . ."*

My mind flashed back to what had
happened at the Temple. My suspicions about
the current Mashiach, although confirmed
through her sacrificing of Thusia was now
more solidified for me through Thusia's
writings. The decoded cipher continued:

*"You will know the true Mashiach
because she is the opposite of Nebo
who wrote only of the good of mankind.
She will be known as the "Oben"
The one who helps mankind remember the
atrocities
So the people will never forget.
She will be the last of her kind:
A preserver and Saviour of humanity . . ."*

I placed my hands behind my head and
proceeded to fall backwards off my
levitating chair. Deciding to float, I laid
on my back to ponder what I had just
learned. Looking up at the ceiling, I
processed out loud, "So if the Mashiach is
not the true Messiah, then who is *this*
imposter? Even more perplexing, who is the
authentic, 'Chosen One'?" I was hopeful that
if Thusia's predictions proved right, then
this meant that the true Messiah was alive
and in existence. This truth played out
would change the new Heaven and new Earth
transforming it to its intended purpose; an
Eden of peace calling all of creation to

fulfill the autonomy of the individual and freedom of expression. Because I have been in hiding for so long and afraid for my life, I cannot tell you how much this thought thrilled me.

Exhausted, I whistled for Anesi to come to me so we could rest for a while in my bed together. I cuddled under my blankets while Anesi made a nest in my hair. My body responded to the massaging effect of Anesi's tiny hum of a lullaby. I felt each muscle slowly relax, but my mind continued to race. Anesi had sung himself to sleep. His song was replaced by the rhythmic sound of a snore. Instead of counting sheep, I decided to count each inhale and exhale originating from Anesi's rib cage reminding me that in this moment, even Thusia still breathes. "1 . . .2 . . .3 . . . ." Sleep finally engulfed me.

....

When my lungs took in air warm fur graced the inside of my nostrils. My eyes opened to long whiskers wiggling, and two beady eyes looking back at me.

"Good afternoon, Anesi! What have you been up to?"

I let out a yawn and then a snicker when I realized Anesi could not answer me. His cheeks were packed full of his favorite morsels. As he mumbled some sort of sound, crumbs tumbled out of his minute mouth and landed in my eyes. It was as if I had been in a sandstorm. The stinging sensation was enough to motivate me to get out of the bed.

The prospect of finishing the last of the decoding was on the horizon.

"This calls for an 'alotta-choca-expresso" I said sluggishly. Getting my nights and days mixed up was giving me a bit of a headache which meant I had to get out "the big guns." Besides, the caffeine would help my endurance on the last leg of Thusia's work which had proven to be fascinating.

As I came to the end of decoding the manuscript, and realized how revolutionary and dangerous this archive was, I was in a more serious predicament if someone had found me out. The consequences of being discovered with this knowledge in my possession would mean thousands of deaths!

Thusia's scroll was feeding me more wisdom than Counselor Modsiw could ever dish out in the ear of the current Mashiach. I collapsed with the thought of the pure chance of what had been revealed to me. The last section of the scroll concentrated on the revelation of the true, living Mashiach:

*"The Desponsyni can be traced through
the chalise of Mary Magdalene-
From the time of Jesus to the current age
known as, 'The Second Coming!"
I predict she will be revealed
after the years of peace have been
established."*

In the reading of these words, I realized that before the war of Armageddon, Thusia had predicted this exact moment in history. Little did I know how much of a part I would play in the events to change the world's current trajectory. I could not have foreseen just how accurate Thusia was:

*"The Desposyni in future generations
is revealed only to a select few
and is known as: The Secret Daughter's
Society.
There will be a time when the blood line of
Mary disappears in history.
Unexpectedly-She will rise from
the one known as the seed of atonement!*

I sleeplessly dug deep, researching back into the historical archive. I was determined to find out 'the seed' Thusia's prophesies referred to. All my work of deciphering came to this unbelievable moment. If I could find out the name of 'the seed' then I could follow the genealogical line to the Holy One. It struck me that somehow Rebekah must have known. Isolation and fear gripped me while adrenaline pumped through my veins. Hidden prophesy was about to give up its secrets.

My hand was trembling and my heart stopped as the last words of the cipher revealed who "the seed" was. I compared it to my genealogical findings. It read:

*". . . the woman whose full name means 'seed
of atonement.' Her sacred blood line will
bear fruit to one named 'saved.' From her
chalice, the Phoenix rises; the true Holy
One!"*

I traced my finger down the names
listed in the family tree of the records I
had researched. My finger rested under the
revealed name of the Mashiach. Disbelief
overtook my body. Tears began to stream down
my face. My lungs drew in a sudden gasp that
startled me. I felt the life leave my limbs
and my face drain to white. All my senses
transcended into unconsciousness.

THE PLAN

"The light shines in the darkness and the
darkness has not overcome it . . ."
(NIV, John 1:5)

I only had three days to strategically
come up with a way to rescue Thusia. I was
reminded June 6th was quickly approaching
every time I turned on my holovision. While
the city was busy preparing for the arrival
of the Mashiach, I was anticipating being
able to hold Thusia in my arms, feeling her
living breath again. This was my second
chance to make everything right.

My covert operation would be so much
easier if I had someone to help me. Already
being in hiding, I knew this was not an
option. Just for fun, I might consider
taking Anesi, my loyal companion, to boost
my confidence, and not feel so alone in the
task. "A plan implemented well is one that
is thought through over and over with all
the possibilities of the what if's."

"Do you really believe that?" Anesi
piped up.

I must have said those words out loud
without realizing it.

"You will dig yourself a hole with the
what if's. Do not go down that road unless
you want to stay in a place of second
guessing yourself. Have confidence in what
you know, and go for it."

I knew Anesi was right! Thusia's life
was worth a plan based in my confidences.
That is where I needed to put my time and
energy. I thought, *Ze, if there was ever a*

time I needed you, this is it.

I could not help myself. I was in what if mode. Despair started to rise from my toes and land in my throat. *What if I don't succeed?* The only activity that would break this cycle in my thinking was to take a Ziggurat break.

Yes, my mind will clear and I will come up with an iron clad plan. Not only will I rescue Thusia, but I will get rid of the Mashiach who is nothing but an imposter. I am determined to find out who this person is. I am convinced Phineus knows. As a backup plan, I will keep him alive so I can find out what I need to know.

The heaviness of the situation came over me with a seriousness I could not shake. I challenged myself to take on the mindset of a secret agent with nerves of steel, poised with clarity of mind. I always admired the air of confidence projected by a 007 type. I wanted to know what it felt like to enter a room, and have complete control of the environment.

Raised high in the sky in my Ziggurat, the large glass encasement testified to the beauty of the new day. This created an atmosphere for determined thinking, and a space for a solidified game plan. I aimed the telescope towards the Temple in the distance bringing it closer to view with an adjustment of the lens.

I thought back to the day I was there, and relived it in my mind. The place where I had stood behind the glass tree was the perfect position. I would keep that part of the narrative the same. The location will give me strategic access to two important elements: the Pitahui and the Mashiach.

(Side Note: What I haven't shared with you up to this point is that I have eidetic memory.)

What I remembered from that day was the whistled tunes Phineus used to call the Pitahui in the square, and the precise pitches he whistled to direct the bird to the poisoning of Thusia. I put that important information to memory knowing somehow it would come in handy. This time, when the bird lands in the tree above my head, I can signal the whistle for the bird to come to me. I will capture it in a metallic box. I plan to, ahead of time, create a hologram of the Pitahui. When I capture the real side kick of Ophis Phineus, I will replace it with the bird's hologram sitting on the branch. Phineus will be none the wiser.

I shifted the telescope to the huge wooden doors, the gateway to the inner courts.

I should be able to travel more gracefully this time retracing my steps up to the Temple mound. I think that part of the journey will be without worry. I convinced myself staying undetected was not hard. Besides, this time, I have the advantage of knowing what is going to happen having already lived it once in the future.

I heard the *psshh-psshh* sound of Anesi's H-pack echoing up through the tube of the Ziggurat. His cuteness landed on my right shoulder.

"Howzit go'in'?" Anesi said munching on

some crunchy goodness. Opening my mouth to answer, Anesi didn't give me time to reply. He plopped into my mouth a savory treat and forced my lips shut around it with his tiny paws.

"You better keep your strength up. Now continue devising your evil plan and I'll check on you later."

I found myself not being able to argue. Anesi was my biggest supporter right now and I needed it.

As I used my telescope to gaze into the sky, I contemplated the secrets concealed in the inhabitants of the nine moons, and the events leading up to the reign of the fake Mashiach who was responsible for the drugged obedience of humanity. My angered thoughts surged over the capture of Thusia. The fate of the new Heaven and the new Earth cannot continue in such a corrupt system. My calling, although difficult, compels me to act.

It would be important this time upon entering the Temple, for me to find a way to Dr. Muse's laboratory. My two weapons of choice would be to retrieve Rebekah's holotrol, and her special glasses. These will come in handy in my plan to distract Ophis and subdue the life feeders. I know my approach will not be flawless, so having more than one weapon in my line of defense will be crucial.

I was so deep in thought I barely noticed the hovercraft that flew by my telescope way too close for comfort. I did not give my usual explicative when such aircraft would fly by blocking my view of the stars. Most flying craft were zoned for lower altitudes, but space flight vehicles associated with the nine moons have special access. Knowing the truth, that they cater to the elite, makes my blood boil.

With much more speed than I had anticipated, I gave a gigantic push with my arms propelling myself down the cylinder passageway into my apartment. I found my anger to be highly motivating.

At this point, I was feeling quite confident about my plan. To create a safe enclosure for the Pitahui, I would need to secure a chain to the metal box. This way I could wear it around my neck to keep my hands free. I looked everywhere in drawers and boxes trying to find chain links and my welder. I always did think more clearly while doing kinetic activity.

After collecting all my supplies, I set to work preparing the special cage that would secure my weapon of choice for bring-ing down Aadah Nakal. As sparks flew in every direction, and feeling the heat on my face, I could not help to think what that moment would be like.

Tell me who you are! What is your real name? I practiced these words over and over in my mind knowing that this would be my first time ever considering the taking of another person's life. I shudder even sharing these words with you now because it goes so much against my character, every-thing I've been taught, and everything I believe in. But justice and righteousness draw me to this conclusion for salvation to come. *Before the poison of the Pitahui takes*

you, reveal yourself! Who are you? Beads of
sweat dripped onto the tiny metal box making
a repeated pinging sound like the count down
before a rocket launch. The only hope that
held my nerves together was the thought of
saving Thusia. I continued to strategize my
moves.

Once I've gathered the holotrol, and
glasses, I'll make my way to the worship
space where everyone will be gathered. I
must make sure I have a shroud to hide my
identity. When the timing is right, Thusia
will descend and land on the alter, the
Mashiach will give her blessing, Thusia will
read what I now know are not her last words,
and then Ophis Phineus will signal the
hologram of the Pitahui sitting on his
shoulder to fly to Thusia. In that moment
when the Mashiach realizes the Pitahui is a
fake, I will yank the golden cord bringing
the Mashiach down to the ground. I will
activate my hologram to sit on top of the
supposed 'Holy One'. I will grill the
counterfeit Messiah hoping to find out her
true identity before the poison penetrates
and drains the life from her. It will be the
end of a farce.

In the minutes proceeding the
confrontation, it will appear I have only
been present in the room as a bystander, but
in reality, I will release the real Pitahui.
I will use Dr. Muses' glasses to spray the
neuro-inhibitors as I make my way through
the crowd to Thusia. In the confusing
circumstances, people will be stunned and
bewildered. I'm hoping most of their
attention will be drawn to the Mashiach

interacting with my hologram. The
distraction will give us time to exit the
Temple without notice. Our grand escape will
further benefit from the advantage of
nightfall.

I looked out the window, and with the
sight of darkened sky I shivered at the
thought that all of this would be taking
place in only two short days. I would use
this time to mentally prepare myself as best
I could. Staring in the distance, I wondered
where Thusia was, if she was alright. I
still don't know what events perpetrated
Thusia's capture by the Mashiach. I too had
to consider the possibility of the danger of
that fate befalling me.

I never wanted the role of hero or
martyr. Somehow the healing of a system
always seems to demand one. It might as well
be me.

....

I can understand that the information I
am sharing with you is quite disturbing. It
is practically my written confession of
murder. But I would implore you not to turn
a blind eye to the larger situation at hand.
It is my sentiment *that* way of thinking,
turning a blind eye, is what causes our
world situation in the first place. And
thus, one of the events I am trying to warn
you against is the repeated atrocities of
history that are passed down through the
generations. You might think I'm talking
about greed, war, or genocide but I am not.
I'm trying to wake you up to one of the
worst being- in the midst of injustice,

doing nothing.

THE RELEASE

"Courage is a kind of salvation." Plato

Surrendering to the playfulness of nature, the wind danced and sang as it pushed the clouds back like the opening of stage curtains revealing the dawn of a new day. Sunrays beat warmly on my face reminding me of the strength that comes from light. There was comfort in hearing the repeated morning routine of thumping at my door.

On cue, I pressed the button for the release at my entrance, letting Anesi in. Rolling around in his hover ball, he seemed excited not taking any time at all to connect to his labyrinth, eager to get to me. "Weee!" Anesi flew out of the tube arms and legs splayed as if diving off the high dive. All I could think was, *I hope I have as much courage as Anesi, anticipating the events of the day.* June 6th had arrived.

I took my time preparing every detail. The night before I meticulously laid out the linen shroud I made. Two pockets, one designed to carry Anesi and the other to hold the holotrol graced each side. I examined the metallic box making sure it was the right size to accommodate Phineus' flying foe. My body reflexively breathed in. I was determined to concentrate on each step, in full vision, with precision to the plan. My eye was on the prize-Thusia.

My goal was to get up slowly, intentionally listening to what my body was telling me. In my intellect, I felt strong and ready but my stomach was slightly twisted, clearly not in any condition to eat. *A shower is always relaxing*, I thought as I grabbed a towel, humming my favorite tune, and hearing Anesi from behind mimic me in tow.

"Where are you going, little buddy?" I asked giving Anesi a curious look.

"I've got to get ready too. You are my Sensei, my mighty leader."

"No sucking up, alright? Now stay out here while I prepare for the most important day of my life."

Anesi could not believe I closed the door in his face. I gave myself needed time to think about how, from this day forward, my life would not be the same.

The warm water blessing the crown of my head felt more like a baptism cleansing me of my sins before they had even been committed. Any sense of guilt, shame or hesitancy washed down the drain, and I was left with quiet resolve to do what was right. My conscious was clean.

I turned the faucet to the off position. *If only I could turn off my vulnerability just as easily*, I thought standing motionless with water dripping from my body; my face. It was as if tears emanated from every pore of my skin before any act had been committed. Stepping out of the aqua-dome I experienced pressured air hitting my epidermis at different levels raising my consciousness to my human-ness. Guilt and shame started to well up to the surface like Adam in the garden of Eden. I suddenly felt a need to cover my nakedness.

Methodically, I placed each of my arms in my fitted white, linen, shroud. In one pocket, I place my holotrol that held the pre-made hologram of the Pitahui. The other pocket was filled with Anesi, who would play the role of a spy entering the land of Canaan. Like performing a priestly ritual, I held up the chained metal box and placed it over my head noticing the necklace length caused the little box to lay against my chest at heart level. *Thusia is depending on me*, I thought. My determination strengthened.

I turned on my holovision to make sure there would be no error of timing on my part. Carisse Nuvo was reporting live at the plaza . . .

"The crowd is beginning to gather for this momentous occasion. The electricity in the air exemplifies the excitement of catching a rare glimpse of the Mashiach. We will be here all morning giving minute by minute live coverage . . .What? Okay . . .I've just heard from our producer, the Mashiach will be here in only two short hours. Now back to you, Cory."

I decided to take one last look in the mirror to give myself a visual cue of anything I may have forgotten. As I slowly drew my hood up over my head, I fixated my eyes on my gaze. In that moment, I realized what was different from my experience in the library. This time, I had a reflection of my true self.

....

On route to the plaza, my senses took on superpower strength. My hypersensitivity served as a protective mechanism to blend in with the crowd. "Take it easy," I told myself *No reason to be paranoid. Just pace yourself.* All I needed to do was act normal. *I've got this,* I reminded myself as a thought of Thusia renewed my confidence.

I made my way through the crowd to the base of the glass tree where I had stood before. Only this time I would be more in control of the state of events. Anesi looked up at me from the bottom of my pocket, and without saying a word gave a thumbs-up. The atmosphere was festive, with music lifting my nervous energy. A series of popping sounds grabbed the attention of the crowd who broke out with applause in response to the beauty of colorful fireworks breaking overhead. It signaled only thirty minutes before the Mashiach would appear before the people in a majestic parade full of pomp and circumstance.

Waiting was agonizing. I decided to pass the time by thinking of Thusia and repeating my mantras. My eyes were squeezed shut, and my lips moved as I whispered them over and over to myself. Suddenly, I felt Anesi poking my side. This woke my sleeping ears to distant drums.

I turned to look over my shoulder to see the crowd section by section going down on their knees as the Mashiach passed by. I hid behind the glass tree of life pressing my back hard against it, trying my best not to hyperventilate.

This is it! This is my only chance!
The vibration of the drum beat was felt in every sinew where bone meets bone. There was no way to deny the reality of the moment. The droning and thumping of the mallet on animal skin outweighed the striking of my heartbeat wrapped in human flesh. The crescendo, now crushing my eardrums, came to a sudden stop at the front of the outer gate of the Temple. The crowd around me obediently bowed as I continued my hiding position poised for action.

I trusted the sudden silence in the air. I closed my eyes and held my breath. I waited . . .There it was right on cue! My soul leapt at the sound of fluttering wings that landed on the branch above my head. *Not too soon . . .wait for it.* The Pitahui predictably began its melodious dirge, only this time to be sung for the demise of the Mashiach and not Thusia. It was time to make my move. I pursed my lips, *Whhheet-wa-wwrreet!*

I whistled simultaneously opening the box I had crafted. I made sure to stand as still as I could because there was no room for error. The Pitahui came to me perching its feet on the box's edge.
So close . . .almost there! Now what? I thought as I stood at attention like an obedient soldier. I heard a *tink, tink* sound in the bottom of the box that created a slight vibration. I froze. The Pitahui hopped in after it. I quickly closed the top and clasped it; not quite understanding what prompted the Pitahui to jump inside. I had no time to waste.

I grabbed the holotrol, aimed it at the branch, and turned it to the *on* position. There in flawless realism, flapped the orange-bellied bird in all its glory. The Mashiach was waving to the crowd with Counselor Modsiw flitting around like a magic pixie. Any minute, I should hear Phineus prompting the entourage along.

Whhheet-wa-wwrreet! Right on cue! The hologram bird flew off and landed on Phineus' shoulder. Ophis' urgency for the safety of the Mashiach caused the life feeders to pick up the golden cord to continue the procession. This was the opportunity to make my move.

Everything repeated like a great cosmic doppelganger. I could not believe how smoothly everything was going by plan. This time every step I took to the entrance to the Temple was one step closer to Thusia's freedom. I was focused and ready.

This must be what being a hero feels like. It is not the absence of fear, but facing it, and coming out stronger on the other side. From the inside out, I had a sense of calmness and authority that spilled over because I knew what to do when I heard the Mashiach's platform lower to the ground inside the Temple doors.

....

The Temple was pitch black as before with only a hint of candlelight glimmering from the worship space at the end of the long hallway. Rebekah's laboratory was in the opposite direction. I purposefully let go of the golden cord and fell to the back of the crowd.

"Ok, Anesi, my great warrior, I am relying on your stealth and speed. Just at the entrance into the worship space is a large stone statue. Hide yourself there. Be observant of the order of events. When you see the descending of candles come and get me. The timing is of utmost importance."

I gave Anesi a peck on the head, lowered him to the ground, and off he flew weaving in and out of the life feeders' feet making his way towards the opening of the worship space. With bravery, I turned completely around, and silently made my way in the opposite direction.

Once in Rebekah's laboratory, I was careful not to turn on the lights or make any sounds. I groped in the darkness to find the holotrol that held the hologram she had made of me. This will serve as one of the main deceptions to aid Thusia, and me in getting out safely.

I also needed to find the special glasses containing the neuro-inhibitor. I knew I would be wearing these so I purposefully did not attach goggles to my shroud. Dr. Muse's special glasses would serve me well as my 'goggles.' I could not help but think of those early days when Dr. Muse aided me back to health in this very room. I was so swayed by her kindness. My thoughts snapped back, *not everything is what it seems.*

This part of my plan was not so easy. It was taking too long. I kept bumping into lab equipment and feeling my way as if I was blind. I put my hands in my pockets in frustration. My right hand landed on the holotrol. "Of course, Why didn't I think of that before?" The holotrol, when in the position between *off* and *on*, emits a light. I clicked it to the half way mark. In anticipation of Anesi coming, I hurried about the room quickly finding the goggles in a cabinet above Rebekah's desk, and the holotrol in her lab coat pocket. Slipping the goggles over my head was like putting on a new perspective. I thought, *Soon Thusia will experience freedom.*

A sound made my heart skip a beat. My feet froze and from the corner of my eye, I caught the movement of a shadow at the front door of the lab. I held my breath waiting for the door knob to slowly turn. Instead, the shadow bounced from the light of my hologram onto the wall moving first to the right, then to the left, past the door creating a huge monster-like shape I could barely make out. When my mind stopped playing tricks, I exhaled and realized it was only Anesi outside the door signaling me it was time. I turned the holotrol to its *off* position, adjusted my glasses, and quietly opened the door.

Anesi was careful not to speak, but pointed his tiny finger in the direction of the worship space. I looked down the long dark hallway, and saw dancing candlelight at its end. I stared into space for a moment with the thought, *This is it! It's time.* I mustered up every bit of confidence, even though this was probably the hardest thing I have ever done. It was the most rewarding. Before I took my first step, Anesi grabbed the hem of my shroud, athletically climbed up, and landed in my pocket. I could imagine him peeking his head out, placing one paw on the edge of the pocket while authoritatively pointing with his other paw yelling, "Charge!"

....

Hiding behind the statue that stood at the entrance of the archway leading into the inner worship space I could see the shrouded strangers bearing lit candles and putting their attention on the ritual holograms animated with song and show. I slipped into the back of the room scoping the perimeter, calculating my distance from Phineus, and the Mashiach, Aadah Nakal. My breathing became a focal point centering on what was about to take place. I looked up.

Oh, God! I want to see Thusia alive again. My spirit could not contain the thought, and emotions started rushing to the surface like a geyser about to blow. My eyes strained. *Yes!* The first appearance of the deep crimson shroud began to appear flowing downward. It grew above our heads, and she spiraled descending like a beautiful angel given as a gift from heaven. She lightly landed on the altar piece.

All according to plan, I thought. It was so tempting to shout my presence, and rescue her in that moment. Restraint became almost unbearable. Like any successful warrior who waits in the shadow for the right moment, I knew I had to wait only a little longer to make my move. The next few minutes were predictable, and the drama unfolded like clockwork. The movement of the life feeders encircled Thusia, the Mashiach blessed her, and asked for her last words. As Thusia pulled the scroll from her robe an uncontrollable smile came to my face because I knew the truth. These would not be Thusia's last words. They were the beginning of a new dawn. The thought of giving her new life created tears in my eyes, tears of hope, love, and joy! I was strengthened in what should have been a moment of fear and trembling.

" . . .May the generations who fought for freedoms of expression before me, and those who continue the fight after me, prevail above all powers that be to suppress them."

The phrase signaled my sudden rush to the front. With my fingers grasping hold of the golden cord, I yanked with all my might. With a sudden specific force, the Mashiach was brought face down to the ground. A gasp was heard from the life feeders confused by seeing their sacred leader prostrate on the floor. Out of my left vision, I noticed Phineus in a swift motion removing his goggled hood, and yelling in disbelief, "Aadah!" Thusia with amazement written on her face sat up on the alter watching what was unfolding.

In the same moment, the Mashiach got back on her feet. Phineus whistled his signal for the Pitahui. The bird rose from Phineus' shoulder, and faithfully flew towards Thusia. The enchanted beauty of the bird caused Thusia to put her hands out to receive it. The Mashiach clapped, and smiled seeing her plans unthwarted. The bird landed gracefully. It proceeded to hug its wings around Thusia's hands. Thusia was so moved she bent over, kissed it, looked up, and smiled with life in her at the Mashiach.

"What is happening?" Aadah's voice erupted.

Phineus' face was priceless in his stupor. "I don't understand!" he said looking perplexed.

Whhheet-wa-wwrreet! I whistled simultaneously opening my Pandora's box. Like a phoenix, the real Pitahui rose. Setting its sights about the room, the life feeders panicked, and started darting around the room to escape the swooping bird. In that moment, the Mashiach had turned, and put her attention fully on me. Not wanting to hide my identity I took off my hood, placing the glasses atop my head. Thusia let out a cry full of returned love, and disbelief that I was there.

"You!" Aadah Nakal said with anger and disgust. I made the mistake of looking directly into her eyes. My gaze was unwillingly fixed, and my body became heavy unable to move. The Mashiach possessed a hidden power. Anyone who looked directly into her eyes became invisible. While in that invisible state, a person was subject to paralysis.

Thusia, realizing what had just happened, called out to me, "Where are you?" Unable to move, I was defenseless to answer. Chaos continued around me as the Pitahui teased and taunted each moving target in the room. But the Mashiach had her sight aimed

at me. Thusia scanned either side of her.
With a swift motion splitting the air, I
heard the thud of heavy metal on flesh.
Thusia had noticed the Menorah standing
beside the altar, and used it to hit the
Mashiach over the head. Her quick thinking
broke Aadah Nakal's powerful gaze.

"I'm free! Thusia thank you!"

She moved towards me, and grabbed one
elbow, "Are you alright?" I smiled hearing
words flowing from her breath.

Weighted footfalls slapped hard against
the cold stone floor. The Mashiach with
almost super human strength, back in motion,
did not want the poison of the Pitahui to be
her demise. Knowing most people were afraid
to enter the Holy of Holies, she ran into
its supposed sanctuary.

With determination, Thusia looked at me
and said, "Do what you came here to do!"
Without hesitation or fear, I followed the
Mashiach into the forbidden zone, not sure I
would survive to come out alive.

It took a moment for my eyes to adjust
to the modest illumination of light in the
most holy place in the Temple. Unlike the
worship space, this room had no windows.
Looking about the room the periphery was
quite dark, with an alter-like table in the
center of the room. Three ornate, jeweled
boxes sat on top with a majestic tone. I
recognized them as the three gifts of the
Magi; frankincense, gold and myrrh given to
Jesus at his birth.

I had only heard rumors that they
existed in the Holy of Holies. They had been
given to the early Christ followers by

Jesus' mother, Mary, a few years after his death on the cross. As I gazed in astonishment, I could not believe I was in the presence of the very treasures touched by Mary and Jesus. Surrealism almost took over. I remembered learning that one box held incense, another box held manna, and the third, unbelievably housed the Holy Spirit. This was done during the destruction of Solomon's Temple to preserve the essence of worship that would come again during the time of the rebuilding of the current Temple.

I reached out my hand. My fingers traced the intricate carvings of ivory that sang in harmony with gold leaf, ruby, and sapphire.

"Don't touch that!" a hissing tone demanded from one corner of the room. The Mashiach stepped out of the hidden shadows.

Sensing I had the advantage, I placed both hands on the precious boxes and noticed her footsteps stop. With my head bowed, I proceeded, "I know who you are not. *You* are *not* the real Mashiach." I continued with confidence. "Stop your fakery! Tell me who you really are!" My hands began to slowly slide the boxes intertwining them in figure eight motions, mixing them up to demonstrate my power in the moment. I heard Aadah Nakal take a forced gulp in her throat.

THE RUACH

"He will baptize you with the Holy Spirit
and fire."
(NIV, Matt. 3:11)

"Who am I?" Aadah barked back in
indignation. Her diminutive look transformed
into a prideful stance. "Why, I am the
Chosen One, the one who gives life to all
the people, *The* Holy One."

Caressing one of the sacred boxes, I
suddenly opened it revealing the Holy manna.
I replied, "If you are truly The Holy One,
turn this manna into stone!"

"I have nothing to prove to someone the
likes of you . . . You are nothing but a
lowly worm!"

I continued, "It is written, 'Man shall
not live on bread alone, but on every word
that comes from the mouth of God.'"

"It is written? It is written?" She
snarled. "You go against the new Earthly
law. The written word is forbidden. It is
you who is guilty of treason here, not me."

I slowly moved to the next box, first
admiring its beauty. I gestured to open this
one more cautiously more slowly. I could
sense the Mashiach trembling in anticipation
of the unknown. The release produced a
heavenly scent of incense. I picked up a
candle from the altar to light the fragrant
transporter of prayers. The smoke rose like
a serpent.

"If you are the Messiah of the second
coming, cause the smoke of the incense to be
drawn to you."

The Mashiach ignored the request and retorted back, "It is also written (playing my game now), 'Do not put the Lord your God to the test!'"

Realizing the last box was left to open, Aadah began to squirm. She attempted to lunge towards me, and I abruptly grabbed the last precious box securing it in my arms. She took a step backward, and I placed the Magi treasure in front of me on the altar.

"I'll ask you one more time . . .Who are you?" My hands on the clasp, I expected her to tell me.

"I will give you all of this, and tell you my name, if you will step away from the altar."

Insistent I said, "Who . . . are . . .you?"

From the depth of her soul came a blood curdling laugh that brought chills to my bones. The Mashiach's laugh reminded me of Dr. Muse's laugh in the library. Only one second lapsed between her evil cackle and my response.

"Get away from me Satan!" I commanded.

My hands unclasped the golden box dressed with Seraphim. The Mashiach had a look of horror as I pulled back the lid opening the jaws of the third and last box. With a force that knocked me to the ground, the roaring *Ruach* gushed forth in the form of a flaming fire. Instead of feeling heat, it brought with it a chill in the air that caused me to tremble uncontrollably. My eyes widened as I witnessed the intentional nature of Holy Spirit fire completely consume Aadah Nakal before she could even utter a scream. Her formless robe lay lifeless on the floor.

With adrenaline surging, my mind went back to Thusia and her safety. Feeling my feet steady beneath me, I ran back to the worship space. I stopped in my tracks. My body reflexively stepped backwards; not being able to compute the information that my mind was trying to process. I saw the mighty rushing flame that had spit forth from the Holy of Holies like a ferocious dragon, now dance above Thusia's head, and surround her like a protective fortress.

"Thusia," I yelled unsure of how to get to her. She ran towards me. My hands went up to shield my face in anticipation that our union would have disastrous consequences. I felt her hand grab mine, and with her other hand she embraced me. I opened my eyes unharmed and in the protection zone. Every now and then we could see the glowing faces of the life feeders through the flames, and hear a disheartening zapping noise. We soon realized the life feeders' attempts to get to us were in vain. They would touch the life force of the Holy Spirit and instantaneously turn to ash. After a while the zapping sounds fell silent. There was not much movement left in the room, only the fire breath of God that delicately danced around us.

"Thusia, are you alright?"

Crying she answered, "Yes! I cannot believe you came for me. You saved my life. Thank you!"

"Do you know what happened to Ophis

Phineus? Did he hurt you?"

"No, no . . ." She pointed as her words faded. I looked to my left. Phineus lay dead, motionless on the floor. I looked away, and then peered back not believing what I was seeing. The Pitahui's body covered Phineus' mouth with dripping wings hugging his cheeks. Seeing his eyes fixated wider than normal with fright, I realized his cries for help were muffled; silenced. A sound came from the back of the room interrupting the disturbed scene.

Thusia and I watched as the traveling fire of the Holy Spirit left us to engulf and penetrate the polished black marble walls of the Temple. In contrast to the death-telling story of the memorial walls, the breath of life poured into each etched name. The inscriptions, like apparitions, transformed into their original beings, and were literally raised from the dead. At first, we could see faint whispers of ghostly hues that grew into flowing figures that walked out from the walls. My mind tried to comprehend what seemed impossible. The Holy Spirit created the living from the dead. Before our eyes, each entity drew in their first breath of resurrected life. This generation was truly born again.

Thusia and I were part of the host of witnesses experiencing the Holy Spirit's filling of the Temple with living breathing beings. Without warning, the tornado like force of the flame broke through the holographic Temple windows. The Holy Spirit made its grand escape from the Temple into the new Earth shooting through the air with

such a force that it left a trail like a
comet. Thusia and I ran to look out beyond
the broken pieces of colored glass. The Holy
Fire danced on the heads of the people
waking them from their stupor; asleep no
longer to the Truth.

THE RISING

"The authentic self is soul made visible"
-Sarah Ban Breathnach

Anesi poked the dripping feathered figure one more time.

"Yep, we are safe! The Pitahui is definitely dead!"

Like a warrior waging battle waving his mighty sword, Anesi plunged the pointed tip of a golden cross into the side of the Pitahui making sure Thusia and I were safe. I felt relieved in the moment; my body exhausted and in disbelief of what had just happened.

The fatigue poured over me. I realized that from this point on nothing would be the same. The events that took place here were not just life changing for Thusia or for me, but for the whole world. I could not help thinking, *Once the word gets out, I will not know freedom ever again. But where my freedom ends, Thusia's freedom begins. I would want it no other way.*

Guilt and shame bubbled to the surface. The critic in my mind repeated, *lack of caring about the loss of life of the Mashiach makes you exactly like her.*

I heard out loud in a loving tone, "You will never be like her! You do not have the capacity in you!" She had read the look on my face.

I turned to face Thusia. She continued, "Do you know how I know?"

Tears came to my eyes at the pure intimacy of Thusia knowing my thoughts without me having to say a word. She placed her finger beneath my chin and looked directly into my soul.

"I know because you have the capacity for love, and compassion! You saved my life!"

We collapsed in each other's embrace feeling that no matter what consequences may come, the paradigm had shifted towards rightness. I felt whole in the moment anticipating a better future for humanity. With the full weight of Thusia in my arms, I slid my back down one wall landing lightly to the floor.

I could hardly believe the reality of this moment; living in *my* present, feeling Thusia's breath filling *my* arms, *my* mind and *my* soul. Her presence was so strong. Peace beyond understanding took hold of me as I drifted into an exhaustive sleep.

....

After an unknown amount of time had passed, I half awoke to a repeated knocking sound. I held my hand up instinctively as if holding a remote, and pushed an imaginary button to let Anesi in the front door or so I thought. The sound continued and would not stop. My eyes slowly fluttered open to the reality that I was not in my apartment. The Temple was so quiet. The only movement in the room was the vibration created by the knocking sound coming from the clock mechanism in the Temple tower telling the passing of time, and bringing me back to the reality of the situation.

I panicked when I realized Thusia was not with me. With the light of morning shining through the broken holographic glass, I could absorb finally the reality of the chaos that lay all around me; the cost of change. I decided to peer out the window down into the plaza, past the gates, and into the city.

In the distance, I could hear crowds of people cheering for what reason I did not know. *Were these gangs organizing for revenge or people realizing their new-found freedom from the Mashiach?* My body shuddered in the not knowing.

The blood rushed to my head and I snapped back to the reality of not knowing where Thusia was. I ran down the long hallway towards the lab yelling, "Thusia!" as if my mind could not grasp losing her again.

....

I crashed through the lab door, breathless as if I had been searching for a long, lost puppy or running a half marathon. There, sitting Indian style, hovering just above the ground with Anesi whispering in her ear, Thusia giggled at whatever he had said. He popped a cheesy treat into her mouth.

Her beauty penetrated deeper than her looks, and dripped into every movement of her body, every expression on her face. Her aura was at ease with freedom; with life. I thought, *how can she be so carefree not knowing what lies ahead?* Having her life back, and seeing her so full of joy in the moment negated any negative thoughts for the future.

"Thusia, you scared me! I had no idea where you had gone!"

"Take your hover shoes off gravity mode and stay awhile!" She said in a relaxed tone. "Anesi and I woke up hungry, and decided to look for food. I did not want to disturb your sleep."

At this point, I noticed they both were wearing one of Dr. Muses' medicinal food patches. Anesi's patch ran the length of his back and was about as big as he was.

"Anesi, your patch should keep you fed for a month." I began to smile, and felt the tension leave my body.

"Here, you must be starving!" Thusia said. She eagerly shared her crunchy treat with me. My body craved the physicality of real food in my mouth.

She walked over to Rebekah's lab coat pocket, and brought to me a whole hand full of patches. She picked one out the pile, slowly peeled the adhesive, and lovingly placed it on my arm.

"There, now! You'll feel better in no time."

Little did she know my body and mind already felt better the moment I ran through that door, and saw with my own eyes that she was alive and in my presence.

....

I did not think the timing was right to let Thusia know my intentions. I knew, sooner than later, I would need to leave the

Temple to retrieve the scroll, and, somehow, I would need to figure out a way to influence our future for a positive outcome. This is where I first came up with the idea of using *Alcheringa* time to carry our narrative to the past. My hope is in the telling of our story, we would be able to change fate; the past influencing future events for the good of humanity.

Getting to my hideaway would be risky. My main objective was to keep Thusia safe at the Temple. I would need to venture out alone. I planned to stay with Thusia through the night, and start my journey under guise of darkness the following setting of sun. It sure would be helpful to know the state of affairs in the city before making my quest.

Of course! Why didn't I think of that before? "Hey Anesi, climb up those wires over there and turn on Dr. Muse's holovision. I'm curious to see how the people are responding to the news of the Mashiach's death, as well as the release of the Holy Spirit from the Temple."

At first the holovision emitted nothing but a fuzzy screen and white noise. Carisse Nuvo's voice and face were distorted like in one of those fun mirrors at the fair.

"Come on, come on!" I said impatiently wanting to know; yet not.

Anesi, Thusia, and I were hushed with full attention to the screen when it finally came into focus. Carisse Nuvo was reporting live from the streets of Jerusalem. With tall towers of fire blazing, the crashing of glass could be heard behind her. Crowds covered the streets with different factions shouting maga-phoned mantras in unison. Certain people in the crowd still had traces of Holy Spirit fire dancing above their heads. We could hear them distinctly chanting, "The true Messiah rises, the Mashiach has come! The true Messiah rises, the Mashiach has come!" The angry crowd surged back like a mob retorting, "The Mashiach is dead! Her killer we will behead!" Carisse Nuvo's voice strained above the stress of the community's chaos:

"Here in the streets of Jerusalem you could cut the tension with a knife! Without the leadership of the Mashiach there does not seem to be a sense of direction for the state of the World Order. There are people I have talked to who report off camera they are relieved to be free of the Mashiach's controlling rule over society, and praise the release of the Holy Spirit to finally touch the lives of the people. Others are not so sure this is a positive change. They tell me they will fight to get society back to the old order. (At this point, Carisse ducks, and a ball of fire crashes at her feet with the sound of breaking glass). As you can see, being on the streets is very unstable and unsafe. Back to the station. Reporting live, this is Carisse Nuvo."

Thusia's thoughts of ever being safe outside of the Temple were waning. I felt it was imperative for me to attempt *Alcheringa* for our story to be told, in order to warn against the false Mashiach.

Anesi clicked the holovision off.

"Let's try to stay lighthearted and positive. We are safe here." Anesi climbed on top of Thusia's right shoulder, extended his tiny furry paws to hug Thusia's cheek, and gave her a reassuring kiss.

"We are here for you." I said taking her hand.

"We are in this together!" Thusia said with such a strength letting us know she was there for us too. In reality she was there for all the people, all the world. They just did not know it yet. She would be their Princess of Peace.

....

Have you ever dreamt of a night filled with no cares, no obligations, and freedom to just be in the moment? That is exactly what my last night with Thusia and Anesi was like; pure heaven! I had not felt so much joy in such a very long time.

....

"What I wouldn't give to have a bath right now!" Thusia pined.

Anesi being the observant one said, "Well this may sound crazy, but there is a baptismal font right outside of the worship space."

"Oh Anesi, you are a God-send! Thank you!" And with a quick peck on Anesi's head, Thusia set out with a skip in her step while humming a tune.

It had been so long since I was able to take a deep breath. I decided to create a relaxing atmosphere that night as a surprise for Thusia, and to calm all our nerves. I cautiously entered the Holy of Holies expecting Aadah Nakal to jump out of the shadows. I tried to ignore my body's automatic response of a panic attack as I picked up the jeweled box on the altar containing incense.

I carried it with much reverence into the worship space, and placed it on the altar where Thusia was to be sacrificed. The beautiful candlelight danced with glorious delight off the polished walls of the Temple. It was like getting free entertainment in shadow theatre. The smell of frankincense wafted past my nose. Its path twisted and turned with the smoke drifting to freedom out the broken stained glass windows. The lighting of incense added to the ambiance of the room and I began to relax.

Meanwhile, Anesi was playing around with buttons of a remote he had found which triggered the holograms which prompted music to begin their worshipful tones. Harps and cherubs, seraphim, and winged creatures of various kinds filled the space, and echoed down the hall.

"Thusia should be finished by now." I said wondering what was taking her so long. I decided to check on her.

I went quietly to the archway and without a sound, peeked my head around the corner, and into the room so as not to startle her. When my eyes landed on her bodily form, I tried not to gasp.

Glistening with tiny beads of water

dripping from her soft, sun-baked skin, Thusia stood by the baptismal font like a Goddess full of beauty and grace. I was paralyzed with the power she had over me in that moment. She turned, her back not facing me anymore, and I watched intensely as she dipped her hands into the water as if cupping God's salvation and calling. She released the power of who she was by anointing her head, her face, and her body with Holy water.

"Thusia" I said in almost a whisper not to be too intrusive. My eye's gaze flitted quickly to the cold stone floor contrasting the warmth of the moment before.

"Behold me in my nakedness. Do not be afraid. Nakedness is Truth in its purest form. Truth is vulnerable. Truth is uncomfortable. But Truth will set you free!! For here is where you recognize that I am human and divine just as we all are. With what has happened here at the Temple, we all have the potential now not to just be baptized with water, but with the fire of the Holy Spirit."

I must have been standing there frozen with my mouth dropped open not knowing what to say. Instead I chose to act. Running as swiftly as I could, I dashed to the lab, grabbed Dr. Muse's lab coat, and appeared again in the archway. Without looking this time, I extended my arm into the room holding the white jacket to simulate a robe.

"For you Thusia," I said cautiously.

"You are most gracious. Thank you for your kindness."

Her hand touched mine. In that moment,

I felt a healing power surge through my body
that surprised me. I had never felt anything
like it before. All I know is any doubts,
disbeliefs or lack of faith had disappeared
in the twinkling of an eye. It was all
replaced with hope, love, and extreme
confidence in what was happening.

THE QUEST

"Transforming fear into freedom-how great is
that?"
- Soledad O'Brian

As the spectrum of colors purple, pink,
and orange streaked across the October sky
giving signal to my soon departure, the tips
of my lips arched upward remembering the
sweet taste of laughter, love, and dancing
from the night before. Tonight, would be
different.

All evidence of death and destruction
had been erased from the worship space and
replaced with a night of splendor; just me,
Thusia, and Anesi creating an illusion of
bliss in our fantasy world for just one
night. It was as if God's kingdom was on
Earth in that moment; playing out the
prophecy of no more tears and no more dying.
This would be the hope with the rising of a
new Mashiach-the true Messiah.

I replaced my shallow breathing with a
deep meditation breath, slowly inhaling the
remnants of frankincense in the air. A
flavor sat on my tongue as the fragrance hit
my olfactory glands, and then penetrated my
brain. The calm breeze sailed softly through
the broken window as multiple colors danced
across glass-edged shards, so enticing yet
dangerous in their beauty. The brokenness
was so transparent it continued to tell the
story of what had occurred in the previous
days. I could not help but think that the
Temple windows did not create a wall of
separation anymore but instead could be

thought of as a gateway opening the very power of the Holy Spirit. I had hoped to feel that safety and protection again as I made my way into unknown dynamics of a hostile city to retrieve Thusia's sacred scroll. The thought of the information getting into the wrong hands was too unbearable for me to fathom.

Anesi and Thusia went on a quest to gather materials I might need on my journey to secure my safe return. Traveling by night created its own challenges. It was important to move about in a way not to draw attention to myself. Any source of light was out of the question. The darkest path to travel would be on foot which required me to set my hover shoes to gravity mode. This would be the most logical strategy since most of society hovered at different higher altitudes. Most people activated gravity only for certain special social occasions. I also justified that not as many people would be in the shops, restaurants, and roadways at ground level.

In the corner of my eye, I caught a dark figure. First it was small. Then growing larger in size, flapping its wings it moved towards me with intentional, propelled energy. Before I knew it I felt a punch to my body, a pressure over my head, and I was flat on the floor. I heard muffled laughter as if I were under the covers in my bed.

"What in the heck!" I said shocked and surprised.

Thusia piped up. "Oh, Anesi and I had a bet." She continued, "We found a black shroud for you to wear tonight. Anesi said to me, 'I dare you to throw it to see if T.R.'s reflexes are fast enough to catch it or if it will completely wipe T. R. out!' I personally was hoping you would catch it. . . and so, you did sort of. . . with your head instead of your hands. Anesi, I think I won the bet."

"No way!" Anesi said with a snickered smile plastered to his fuzzy face.

I downplayed the moment realizing their lighthearted play was a way not to have to face the pain of our separation or the unknown of the future. Tying the roped waistband, and raising the hood over my head, my presence was darkened. My identity would be protected by wearing my black religious camouflage. Thusia slipped a weighted backpack over my shoulders complete with an H-pack as a 'plan B' in case I needed in it in an emergency.

"I want you to know you go with my blessing. I feel strongly that the Holy Spirit has gone before you, and you will not be alone." Thusia's divine nature had its way with me. Her resolute powerful projection in her voice stripped away all emotional, psychological, and spiritual walls that laid bare my soul. It was odd how her words exposed such vulnerability in me, and seemed to fill me with such strength that I had never been aware of before. My mind absorbed her spirit filled, God-led blessing readying me for the journey.

....

As I stood on the top of the steps descending into the plaza with the Temple behind me, a soft cool breeze caressed my cheek. It playfully ran its fingers through my hair. The playfulness of the wind accompanied me reassuring that I was not alone. Not filled with people, the plaza seemed so much bigger. The environment presented itself with a ghostly hue. A slight fog lay low to the ground weaving its way through the trunks of the glistening glass trees lit by iridescent lights, and lining the plaza on each side. Conditions were perfect for someone like me trying to hide my identity. I hoped the impending fog would linger long enough during the night, and serve as my alliance to get me successfully to my destination.

Since my view was limited at ground level I decided to look up. In the clearness of the night sky I rotated three hundred and sixty degrees to take in each of the nine moons glaring down on me. It was as if these nine muses knew all my secrets. I felt exposed in the moment. As I stared back at their bulbous bodies hanging against an ebony backdrop, I noticed thousands of pin lights glowing in all their glory from each lunar surface.

They know! I thought as my heart sank into my hover shoes. The elite must have gotten the news that the Mashiach is dead! The potential for a rebellious reaction was sure to be a reality. The powers that be will want to gain control again and maintain a status quo. I would do everything in my power not to let that happen. As I gazed upward, each heavenly body glistened with pinpoint lights in memory of the slain Mashiach. They appeared as new stars in the night sky. I could not help think how such beauty disguised a force of deceit and misuse of power. I was more determined than ever to make my journey, retrieve Thusia's scroll, and make my way safely back to her.

I glided in low air space to arrive quickly at the edge of the city. Many buildings set close together formed dark silhouettes against the night sky forming a path of patterned alley ways perfect for my travels. I stopped to place my hover shoes on gravity mode. One of the most incarnational moments is when one's foot meets the ground-so natural yet so risky. Above me the sky was filled with the movement of aircraft flying, air malls filled with people, and the cosmopolitan night life. I wanted to avoid contact at all cost. The shadow of darkness was my only friend to help me accomplish my goals. Traveling without a light source would not be easy but would be very necessary. I first felt the texture of cold rough brick as my hand met the first wall's edge. I ran my fingers along the belly of the building letting its body direct my path much like a blind man's walking stick.

One hand crossed another as I moved forward. With each step, I found my other senses becoming more in tune to the environment. The amplification of smell, sound, and touch without sight, overwhelmed me at first. My anxiety rose as I had to reorient my brain to interpret what it was experiencing. Suddenly, I lost my footing when my hand reached for its next palpitation of the wall and it was not there.

"Ah, I found the alley way. This is good," I said to myself as I regrouped. Taking a deep breath, I rounded the corner. The wall now changed to a smooth wooden feel. Because the facing had changed, I knew I was truly at the back of the building on the alley side. At timed intervals, the plane would be broken by the outline of a window or door. I had to approach these with caution if an indoor light was on. Most of the buildings seemed abandoned and uninhabitable. Every now and then I would bump into an object that was very large, heavy, and cumbersome. I realized after a while these were trash incinerators used to get rid of trash in an environmentally friendly way. I had almost forgotten about them because they are so out of sight of the public. In the coolness of the night, I did enjoy placing my hands on the sides of these massive beasts providing warmth, at least for a moment.

As I turned the next corner, I noticed one faint street light burning a delicate amber color creating a somber mood. *I must proceed with caution so I don't raise anyone's suspicion.* I crossed the street quickly running into a darkened alley. Placing my back against the wall of what looked like a storefront, I looked back to make sure I didn't blow my cover. I froze and the hairs stood up on the back of my neck.

Were my eyes playing tricks on me? I thought I saw a shadow that moved from where I had just come from, and quickly disappeared behind the incinerator. My mind went blank in fright. I instinctively held my breath without realizing I was doing it. *Stay calm and look again,* my self-talk insisted. I peeled my eyes open, and turned my head to look. *There it is again!* The shadow this time quickly slithered from behind the incinerator, appeared as a human form, and disappeared in the adjacent alley. *Quick! Think of a deterrent. I cannot believe someone is following me!*

Just then, I heard the scream of a chipet who was in the alley giving away the location of the stalker's position. I groped around in the darkness to find anything that would help me in my predicament. My hand came across an empty glass wine bottle hovering near my feet next to the store wall. Before I could make my grand escape, I decided to feel my way along the cold dark wall. Shimmying my body along the building to get to the front of the store, I saw the orange hue of the roadway enough to know what I was going to do next. "1. . .2. . .3. . ." When the number three hit my whispered lips, I threw the bottle across the street in the opposite direction. Sure enough, I saw a shadow move towards the sound of the crashing bottle. I ran with the speed of a jetting airship hitting my trajectory with precision. I quietly opened the back door of the store, and disappeared into the darkened building. My heart was racing, and my hands were shaking. Adrenaline had the best of me.

I was so vulnerable, and alone with the
thought that I was so close to being caught.
Tears began to well up in my eyes. Silently
I just stood there in the darkened store
letting my emotions escape in every drop
that fell.

Once inside the space I realized it had
the smell of abandonment. I was startled by
the street-lit curtain panels flapping from
the breeze with the amber street light
pouring in from the glassless window. I
tried to take a step. Hard objects of
different shapes and textures accompanied a
consistent crunching coming from beneath my
feet. This was quite unusual and a sensation
I was not used to since I usually hovered in
travel. My gait was unsteady, and the
circumstances made worse my ability to
maneuver in the dark. I stopped in my
tracks. I was unnerved at a moving shadow
that danced across the curtains dancing
ghost-like in the dim light streaming in
from the street. The uneasy feeling of
someone following me was growing. My
attention shifted to a strong stench of high
volt whiskey burning the inner lining of my
nostrils. I had the sensation I was not
alone in the room. The alcoholic smell alone
set my tongue on fire, and made my eyes
water. I heard someone in a drunken stupor
mumbling at my feet. Before my throat could
even decide to yelp out a sound, a strong
grasp of a hand wrapped its self around my
ankle, and yanked me swiftly to the floor.
The shock of the situation sent me cascading
downward without any control of my body, my
head hitting the corner of a table on the

way down. At least in my unconscious state,
I had a break from darting shadows, and
unforeseen clutching claws.

....

    I awoke to exploding fireworks going off
in my head. *What just happened? Where am I?*
My hand crept slowly upward to the mountain-
ous knot that brought to reality my demise.
I found it hard to open my eyes at first
because of the brightness blaring from
above. I wondered how much time had passed.
My ears seemed more alert and in tune to the
surroundings. As my eyes struggled to open,
sounds of a crowd chanting in unison became
more apparent motivating my ability to try
to get up. I was in a panic. *I must get out
of here before someone finds me.* My eyes now
slightly opened and with one hand covering
my brow, the reality presented itself. I was
not in the protection of the darkened
abandoned building anymore. Somehow, I ended
up in the middle of the road under a bright
street light. *Aaugh!* With my head feeling
like a ship anchor I tried to move. The
crowd seemed to be getting closer. I could
hear a distinguished call and response ping
ponging back and forth from a solo,
megaphoned voice echoed by an organized
crowd. Thoughts of Thusia surged in my
spirit. My body lurched forward and upward.
Fear gripped me as I maneuvered to find
cover. Taking a chance, I quickly ducked
into one of the shops and blended in.
Breathing heavy I thought, *abandoned
buildings aren't as abandoned as they appear*

to be.
    Across the street, I heard the faint off-tune singing of Happy Birthday. Within the satellite salon of The Space Galaxy Ice Cream Shop, I could see multicolored balloons and bouncing children with all attention on the birthday child. *Great Scenario*, I thought, *the attention on the birthday boy will take any attention off me.* Although dizzy, I managed to enter the ice cream parlor.
    My head injury amplified each giggle and pop of a balloon. My body moved as if I had a hangover even though I had not drunk any alcohol. Upon entering The Space Galaxy Ice Cream Shop, I noticed a shift in mood brought about by the atmosphere. To be around the excited laughter of children lifted my spirits, and temporarily took my mind off my pain. I was surrounded by floating tables dressed in glitter coverings that changed colors when touched by the children's hands. I immediately recognized the theme of the party because each child was dressed in a red fleece shroud that imitated the robe worn by the Mashiach during high holidays. Even the gold coins of her majestic robe could be seen strewn about the tables in the form of shiny wrapped chocolate treats. While some of the boys and girls entertained themselves with the interactive tablecloths, other children were shrilling with delight in the corner of the room. I went to see what all the excitement was about. Floating iridescent bubbles filled the air. As the children blew a soapy substance through a tiny ring, a squeal of

delight would be heard at each pop. When a bubble exploded, a miniature chipet would emerge and run to its new owner.

This was the new trend in advertising. If the commercial companies could get children excited, and wanting to collect their cute little products, then perhaps mom and dad would be convinced to buy the more expensive, full-sized chipet as a house pet. I must say, the kids were thrilled, and completely immersed in the moment.

I managed my way past parents taking pictures. I entered the restroom locking the door behind me. An elongated vanity was lit with multiple bulbs, the likes of movie star status. Laid out in an organized fashion was a wig, different shades of putty, make-up, and lipsticks. *This just might be my ticket out of here,* I pondered. I sat in front of the mirror and decided, *If I want to blend in, being a clown at a child's birthday party is the way to do it.* The purple putty went thick onto my face and acted like a soft wet mask. As it dried, I applied glittery hot-pink eyelashes matching my cotton candy lipstick. Gleaming shiny silver "S" shaped eyebrows were peeled, and placed sideways on my brow. Taking the place of dimples, I skillfully painted the classic clown white face in the shape of two small hearts on each cheek. The last touch was slipping on the silly wig that donned a small polka-dotted pill box hat. The wig was made of laser lights that shot in all directions. The rainbow of colors had a setting allowing them to dance and change to music. The hair piece was so technically advanced if someone ran their hand through the fibers, different musical tones could be heard.

Looking in the mirror, I could not help but think for a moment, *if only Thusia and Anesi could see me now.* I had put so much effort into putting on this mask, as it was very necessary for me to survive the journey. I would have a lot to tell them when I got back. Being a clown at a children's birthday party should not be too hard because most of the time clowns don't need to talk. I can just stand around, smile, and give out balloons until the crowd outside passes through. Then I can make my grand escape. I took a deep breath, and reminded myself my identity was well concealed.

Entering the party scene, I stood behind the mirage of parents, and gathered a few balloons. At first I blended in with not much attention to myself until the birthday boy pointed in my direction, and insisted on coming to see me. All the children reached out and chanted, "Balloon, balloon!" I dutifully smiled, patted the tops of their heads, and gave out balloons. *This is going smoothly*, I thought. Parents began to take pictures which made me nervous but I had to keep my cool. *Just a few more minutes, then I can slip out and be on my way.*

The children started to get restless. I noticed the birthday boy whining for his Space Galaxy ice cream cake in a voice that made my nerves surge with a will to escape my skin. The parents "quick-stepped" to the demands of their wailing child, letting everyone know who was really in control. (Cake and space ice cream for four and five year olds does not hold attention for very long). Out of nowhere the young boy started chanting, "Magic show! Magic show!" Unexpectedly, two of the parents took my hands, and pulled me to the front.

A curly haired lady who must have been the mother hushed the crowd. "Thank you everyone for coming. We have had so much fun this evening. Now, for the highlight of our party! I introduce to you, Marvel the Magic Galaxy Clown!" Applause erupted, and I shrank in disbelief of what was happening to me.

I was aware that because technology had gotten so advanced, younger generations were more interested in vintage or old school ways of practice. Children only heard stories of the way life used to be on old Earth, and they had a curiosity to experience it firsthand. Magic was no exception.

I knew magicians such as Houdini were known for their sleight of hand. I reasoned, *they are only four and five years old. It probably won't take too much to impress them.* I started off by miming. Throwing each hand up with a hard thrust of the wrist, I made it appear I was stuck in an imaginary box. The group began to giggle. I approached the birthday boy, and had him check my hands to see that they were empty. With a quick motion, I reached over his shoulder, grabbed a gold coin from the table, placed it behind his ear, and put it in front of his eyes that widened with delight. I borrowed a napkin from one of the floating tables, and carefully unfolding it, I showed both sides. Holding it between thumb and forefinger in both hands, I would hide my face. Then, slowly raise my clown painted façade, first with a smile, then with a frown, and finally with crossed eyes with great delight of the children.

I ended my routine by pulling a red rose from my shroud sleeve that I had placed there when no one was looking, and offered it to a cute shy little curly-haired girl with glasses levitating in the corner. Magically pulling the thorn-less flower from my sleeve, I tenderly looked at her and said, "A beauty for a beauty!" She gratefully took the rose, and seemed to gain confidence from my attention; so much so, she spontaneously gave me a hug which made me laugh. She ran her tiny hand through the laser lights on my head creating a magical melody.

The night was filled with less fear and more innocence. My spirit was renewed in that moment. Floating in air, I did body rotations maneuvering myself back in front of the group.

Holding one finger up in the air, I indicated my grand escape. I proceeded to mime tying a rope around my waist. Turning my back to the group and facing the front door, I acted like I was playing tug of war with the pretend rope. Finally, whoever was on the other end of the rope won the game because I was out the front door with a final jerking motion. Upon my exit, I looked back with a wave in my hand. The exciting energy of giggling children, popping bubbles, festive balloons, and a beautiful curly headed girl with glasses holding a red rose began to fade. I stood in the middle of the street shaking off the joy I had just brought to others to make room for the seriousness of the mission at hand; to find my hideaway, retrieve the scroll hidden under my bed, and get it back to Thusia at the Temple.

....

The coolness in the air as I found my way back to the alley made the make-up on my face feel heavy like caked on mud that had dried in the sun. Running my hands over the rough surface, I imagined the scary picture of a clown whose face was cracked and peeling. No matter how heinous my look, I decided to leave the make-up and wig on as a protection to my identity. *What would Thusia think of me now?* Traveling by alleyway not many people would see me but if they did, perhaps my disguise would make them think twice about messing with a deranged looking clown. I only had two more blocks to travel to my hideaway that I called home. *I am so close to getting the scroll!* I thought, fighting the anxiety crawling around in my skin. Although I continued to wear the wig, I made sure the lasers were in the off position not to emit light or make any noise. The laser-fibered hair would have made an entertaining flashlight.

A lamplight cast long shadows at the corner of the building where I was standing. This would be the last street I would need to cross with the light exposing me for just a moment. I looked both ways making sure the path was safe.

I heard a sound behind me in the darkness of the alley that accelerated my heartbeat and my stride. I felt out of breath even though I had gone a short distance. I now stood beside the local space junk store where I heard footsteps behind me again. The sound of metal being kicked caught my attention from the alley I had just left. I decided to take two steps peeking my head out from the corner of the building to see further. I leaned my head forward with my body staying in the shadow of the store. In the dark, the space junk made shapes that played tricks on my mind. I strained to listen. Without notice, a huge pressure fell onto my right shoulder, and its fingers curled inward toward my collar bone. A chill ran through me. I was in such shock I could not even eke out a scream. My heart sank. *This cannot be happening. I am too close to my goal!* The thought of failing Thusia was unnerving. The presence behind me moved closer with their hand holding me frozen in time. I could see nothing. I dared not chance running in case they had a weapon and intended me harm. The warm breath on the back of my ear made the hairs on my neck stand up. The stranger parted lips, and began to speak in a whispered tone. "Do not be afraid. I am here to help you!"

My eyes grew wide recognizing the voice. "Hell, Ze! You scared the 'begeebees' out of me! How did you. . ." Ze's other hand made its way quickly over my mouth at that very moment the owner of the space junk building came out to the street to lock up and head home.

From this point on, I did not feel alone. Ze held my hand and whispered, "Follow me!" It was as if the lights were on for Ze or Ze had extra sensory perception because it took us no time at all to finish the journey without incident, straight to the front door of my hideaway. "I hope you don't mind," Ze said to me lovingly, "I thought you could use my help!" I was amazed and stunned that Ze showed up in flesh and blood this time not just in a dream. Knowing Ze was with me made me feel confident I would safely get back to Thusia. I entered the doorway first.

"Ze, you don't know how happy I am to see you! So much has happened! My success in getting the sacred scroll back to Thusia is important for proving the credibility of her prophesies, but also the truth of who she is. Will you help me on my return?"

Ze didn't answer. I turned to look behind me, and Ze had disappeared. I pinched myself to make sure the moment was real, and I was not just dreaming. I felt so alone as if Ze had abandoned me during a time I could have used help in facing the journey back to the Temple. I would have to take a chance to get back to the Temple alone. In that moment, I realized how strong and determined I had been up to this point to reach the scroll and protect Thusia. I was not about to give up now.

....

Upon entering my hide away, my home, I became more aware of how exhausted and dirty I felt from traveling. Although I was there for a specific purpose I decided to put my personal needs first.

The trail of laser wig, butterfly eyelashes, and shiny silver eyebrows laying haphazardly on the floor led straight to the most satisfying shower I had ever had. The colors of cracked smeared makeup streamed down my face and body, creating a swirling rainbow that whirl-pooled as the water settled, and then disappeared down the bottomless drain. Washing off the protective mask, I felt more like myself than I had in a very, long time. The pit in my stomach reminded me of how long it had been since I ate. I made sure to unpack the backpack Thusia and Anesi had prepared for me, and replaced its contents with plenty of food. I checked the H-pack making sure the hydrogen tank was still on full. It would be my ticket to getting back to the Temple before sunrise. Putting my hover shoes back on, I switched them to hover mode instead of gravity mode. I flew to my bedroom like I had done so many times before. Flipping my body upside down, I reached beneath the bed feeling for the familiar shape of the scroll. I let out a sigh of relief. I placed the sacred writing carefully inside my darkened shroud. I completed my prep for the journey.

I thought, *at the Temple I feel so out of my comfort zone. Here, I feel safe and comfortable. Thusia is worth my leaving*

everything I have ever known. With that
assurance of thought, I placed my H-pack on
my back took one long look back, and under
the shadow of darkness propelled myself over
the threshold of the doorway out into the
chill of the night never expecting to come
back again.

As I hovered through alleyways, I
thought about Ze's appearance and its
significance. I exhibited more confidence on
my return reminded by Ze and Thusia that I'm
never really ever alone.

As I entered the Temple court using my
H-pack, I felt the freedom of the dawning of
a new age. Weaving in and out of the
beautifully lit glass trees, I dreamt of
what Thusia would look like standing among
them. I climbed higher in altitude making
the broken windows my portal for re-entry.
Decreasing propulsion, my feet landed
squarely in the worship space. Across the
mosaic floor, my eye's attention followed to
the other side of the room where Thusia
stood with her back to me. My heart skipped
a beat. As she turned to face me, I realized
she was wearing Aadah Nakal's sacred robe.
She must have read the look on my face. Her
words quickly changed the subject in my
mind.

"I put it on because I was cold." She
said recognizing that my seeing her in the
Mashiach's sacred robe might take a little
getting used to. I slowly drew Thusia's
scroll from my black robe, and held it in
the light of Her Divine presence standing
before me.

"Thusia, we need to talk."

THE NAME

"Your name, which I played with so
carelessly, so easily, has somehow become
sacred to my lips."- Coco J. Ginger

Thusia watched entranced as I slowly
unrolled the sacred scroll on the altar
table as if I were unraveling her past and
future in one large stroke. The constellations cast in bronze on the poles of the
scroll rotated in motion as if orbiting
celestial bodies, imitating the passing of
time. I could sense her attention on me, and
her ears perked for listening gave the
signal for me to grasp the moment.

"I'm sure you know by now that I am
thorough in my research. It has been such an
honor Thusia, to hold your work in my hands
and decipher your prophesies. I have been
amazed at your accuracy. But as you know,
the wisdom and knowledge contained in your
cipher holds more telling of the truth than
just a first glance allows. I have tried to
seek out that which seems hidden."

"I would not expect any less of you!"
Thusia said as she glided closer with
intrigue in her voice.

"Discovering the fact that Aadah Nakal
was not the true Messiah caused me to ask
two questions, who was Aadah Nakal, really?
And, if she was not the true Mashiach, who
was?"

Thusia continued to listen intently
with a silence that spoke to her interest.
"Go on." She said as her eyes widened.

"Do you remember the third letter of

the cipher?" I said searching through the cryptic symbols penned on animal skin. "Look here." I said continuing to find the section I was looking for. Thusia drew near and her presence seemed to make the prophesy come alive. "Here, in the section of the revelations you write:

'The Desposyni in future generations is revealed only to a select few
and is known as the Secret Daughter's Society
There will be a time when the blood line of Mary disappears in history
Unexpectedly- she will rise
From the one known as the seed of atonement'"

This information led me on a search for who the Secret Daughter's Society was. I knew my chances of finding it were slim, but I did not give up. I continued following the trail. I was hoping to be led to the revealing of who the true Mashiach was. My quest was not easy. Because the information I was looking for was very old in the historic archive, I had to face the possibility that the written evidence had been destroyed with the old Earth or in the taking over of the New World Order. These were all the scenarios that had crossed my mind. My search only brought to the surface more questions at first. If this secret society was so obscure perhaps it was still around, and had protected the information it knew was so important to the future of humanity.

Believe it or not, my paper trail took me all the way back to the nineteen forties; back to the old Earth during World War II. My underground connections allowed me to have access to old newspaper articles. I looked for any mention of the Secret Daughter's Society. What was important for me to know was how and why this women's organization was formed. The newspaper articles at first glance produced nothing. You'll understand why as I reveal more of the context of the story.

"Most people would have given up with no hope of finding what they were looking for, but not my T.R.!" Thusia proclaimed. I had to admit she knew me more than any other person ever could.

The name of the society created a new direction in my thinking. Where had I been aware of an organization that promoted and celebrated feminism? This question served me well. My research came upon a new religion founded in 2045 A.C.E. centered on the feminine. A small convent called *Bahtmistar* was known for its reverence of Mary Magdalene, and her descendants. Believe it or not, I found a connection between this church sect promoting feminism, and an incident that happened in the nineteen forties.

Thusia's facial expression changed as if I were bringing back into her mind a memory she had not thought about for a long time.

In nineteen forty-five, at the end of the war, the allies made their way through each concentration camp looking for survivors. Their hearts were torn apart, witnessing the ghostly emaciated bodies of the living, walking around among unspeakable horrors. Per primary sources, there were reports of one concentration camp that was different than all the others. It was originally known as Bialystok. But, in the official reports headlining the newspaper, it was referred to as *Die Verlorene Kolonie*, the lost colony. The incident was so extraordinary that the newspapers ran the story for weeks. Scientists, politicians, and citizens of Belarus and the whole Eastern front for that matter, could not explain the strange event that had happened there.

It was written that when allied soldiers arrived at Bialystok concentration camp, not a sound could be heard. All the bunk beds were empty, the kitchen completely still, and no prisoners were found. The only evidence was the charred remains of Nazi soldiers as if something terrible had happened. The discovery was so bizarre and unexpected. No one knew what had become of the prisoners in the camp. The secret hope by account of those interviewed was that by some miracle, the Jews had found a way to escape. One interesting fact about the concentration camp I found in my investigation solidified further my suspicions. Looking at the list of names of the Jewish captors at Bialystok, I realized that they were all women! Then, I thought of the impossible. Could it be that this group of Jewish women found a way to survive? With this thought in mind it was imperative I speak to an inside source at the Church of the Feminine. In my conversation with my anonymous source, there was a reference to a secret society of women who had survived World War II. As a remnant of the Desposyni, this was crucial information well protected by the church. How the group survived is still not known. My research confirmed this group needed protection because they were in possession of the written evidence of the blood-line of Mary Magdalene. This was very sacred knowledge to the Church of the Feminine. This information was to be protected at all cost. Although they were not willing to freely give me any information, my source was willing to confirm any research I had found on my own.

"Thusia, do you remember any mention of family stories passed down in your family about World War II or concentration camps?"

At the mere asking of the question, I could tell I had transported Thusia to another place and time. She had a gleam in her eye that seemed half snuffed out by a slight sadness that sat on her brow, and formed across her lips.

In disbelief, she broke her gaze as if snapping back into the present, and began to speak. "Even as a young girl, I was made to feel very proud of my heritage. I always knew there was something special about it, but I could not put my finger on it."

A weight seemed to rest across her shoulders, "I was told that my grandmother Zera, was killed in the concentration camps." She drew in a breath, and with it her body took a stance of pride.

"Even though I did not know my grandmother, I felt like I did. I was told she was full of strength and was known for caring for others. In the camp, if she had food, water, or clothing, she would always share it and put others before herself. She was well liked, and had many friends." The sadness hid itself for a moment, and I saw a small hopeful smile honoring her grandmother's memory.

"Although my grandmother did not survive, my mother was born in the concentration camp towards the end of the war. She miraculously survived. My mother's name was Yasha. From what I was told, she was taken in by my grandmother's sister, Raziel, and raised by her. I came along in 2055 A.C.E. when my mom was thirty-five years old."

"Thusia, you do know what you are inferring when you say that?"

"Yes, I know . . . time travel of some kind. Someone must have discovered or known about *Alcheringa* time even way back then, and chose to use it. That is the only conclusion I can come to; But, who? . . . how? Those things were never discussed in our family for fear of being discovered as a Jewish remnant. So much was covered up, and not discussed out of fear."

Thusia's words were confirming everything my research had been pointing me to. My finger traced along the elaborate symbols of the cipher looking for a specific section.

"Thusia, we need to read this part of the

prophesy again, in light of what we know:

'The Desposyni in future generations is
revealed only to a select few
and is known as The Secret Daughter's
Society
There will be a time when the bloodline of
Mary disappears in history
Unexpectedly- she will rise
From the one known as the seed of
atonement.'"

I continued, "The Church of the Feminine confirmed for me that the genealogical line I had researched is accurate. When I looked deeper into the meaning of your mother's name, I found that Yasha in Hebrew means, 'to save'. This was a very appropriate name given to her since she survived the very clutches of the Nazis. Her survival was nothing but miraculous considering the circumstances she was born into! Your grandmother's sister, Raziel is to be commended for her deep devotion and protection of your mother. What was most intriguing to me in my research was your grandmother's name, Zera. Can you confirm for me what your grandmother's last name was?"

"Sure, I heard my mother mention it often as if she wanted me to keep it in my heart, and my mind for some higher purpose. Her last name was Kaphar."

I collapsed on the floor in the realization in that moment that all my research was true; confirmed by her very lips.

"Thusia, your grandmother's name Zera Kaphar means, 'Seed of atonement!' Do you know what that means?"

Thusia did not say a word. She wrapped the Mashiach's robe more tightly around her feminine frame. I could see tears form in her eyes. In that moment, she turned away from me as if she did not want me to catch the emotions written on her face. When she turned back around, I was prostrate before her acknowledging in that moment, her power, her presence, her majesty, and her calling. Thusia had a kind of knowing, one of a spiritual sense that placed a tinge of peace in the air rather than surprise.

She touched my shoulder and I lifted my head. In all her splendor, *she* stood before me- the True Mashiach. Going over the details in my mind, I let in a backward gasp realizing there was one tiny bit of information I had completely forgotten to ask. My mind was distracted by the reality of this moment; what it meant for the present, and what it meant for the future.

"My Lordess, there is one minor detail I have overlooked, and my mind will not settle if I do not ask it of you."

Thusia looked at me with great sincerity, and understanding. "You know me so well! You should feel free to ask anything of me!"

"Thusia, in all our time together, I have never asked this of you before. . ."

"Ask," she said with a spiritual tone that began to fill the worship space.

"What is your last name?"

She bent down and placed her finger

lovingly under my chin, and raised my eyes
to meet hers. The Messianic gaze considering
my soul magnetically transfixed the moment.
She cupped her other hand lovingly at my
ear, and whispered. My mind acted as a
roller coaster racing through every past
encounter like a person who sees life
flashing before his or her eyes. My mouth
gasped in disbelief as the last syllable of
her utterance hit my brain. Suddenly a light
switch clicked on. . . "Ze?"

EPILOGUE

LAST ENTRY TO THE READER:

It is hard for me to believe that this will be my very last entry to you. I will not have access to *Alcheringa* time after this moment. It will be imperative for me to demolish my beloved typewriter to guarantee all evidence of my writing is destroyed, and inaccessible. This is necessary to protect my identity from those who wish to harm me.

I have the peace of knowing my writing continues with a life of its own in your dimension, and your time in history-at least this is my hope. There is no way of knowing if my efforts to contact you have truly traveled back in time, and successfully reached you. This is where faith lives for me, in the not knowing, but trusting.

I have only had good intentions for a tranquil future; full of light for humanity living in fullness of its true self. Looking to the past as the place for my story to reside is part of the process writing has given me. Life, in its purest form, releases freedom, gives wings to liberty, and a voice to all of us.

Thank you for joining me on the journey even though it was not of your choosing but of mine, out of necessity for survival. Because I have told my story, I cannot only survive, but thrive. This is my longing for you. If only the strings of time could be plucked, and tuned to the same tone for us to have the chance to meet. Perhaps in another place, in another dimension where all things are possible, our souls will mingle, and create a new story.

I know that this may have been said before, but it is worth mentioning here again. As the type righter, I feel it is my obligation and duty to help you with figuring out my identity. For that, I can only give tiny hints that point you in the direction of looking through a specific lens; the revelations of my writing. I beg you to lean on those detections only.

Draw your senses to the spaces between the words, the time between breaths, and the moment before a foot takes the next step. These are the precious whispers in time that come in the blink of an eye. They must be captured, and listened to just like a young child who eagerly places a conk shell to innocence's ear, and hears the magical wonders of the sea for the first time. That is where the voice lives. The voice of choice resides in the in-between places. Do not let the distraction of words, breath, and steps make you forget it is there.

So, it is in the reading of my narrative. If what has been important to you in the reading of it is getting the facts straight or understanding plot, character, or motive, I tell you as the type righter these elements in the story are all distractions to the Truth. Once you discover who I am, you will understand. I am so obvious on the page of a life.

GLOSSARY

I am providing a list of names and words to help with a deeper understanding, and underlying meanings of names that are intentional on my part as the author. My hope is that it draws you into the narrative that is layered, and allegoric in nature.

Aadah Nakal: in Hebrew Adah means *ornament*. Nakal refers to *being crafty or deceitful*. Aadah Nakal: an *ornament of deceit. (I added an extra "a" in Aadah because I liked the way it looked)*.

Adira: the chant of the life feeders which means *noble, powerful*.

Anesi: refer to the numerology chart life path 3 to research further aspects of Anesi's personality.

Chava: *Mother of all living*.

Counselor Modsiw: the word "Modsiw" is wisdom backwards. This is a clue to the reader that backwards wisdom is associated with the current Mashiach.

Desposyni: according to Wikipedia from the Greek meaning *belonging to the master or Lord.* It is also a reference to those who have the bloodline of Jesus.

Icosahedron: according to Merriam-Webster's dictionary "a polyhedron having 20 faces."

Mahlah Zebach: in Hebrew Mahlah is considered both masculine and feminine. Mahlah means *weak* and Zebach means *sacrifice*. Although the name implies an entity that is *easy to conquer or take from*, this character reminds us not everything is as it seems.

Mashiach: *Anointed, the Messiah*

Ophis Phineus: Ophis in Greek means *serpent*. A supposed meaning of Phineus in Hebrew is *serpent's mouth*. The symbolism implies *malice in nature or an enemy*. This would be the tone I set for the relationship between Ophis and the type righter.

Rebekah Muse: Rebekah means *to tie firmly*. Muse refers to the nine goddesses created by Zeus.

Sycophant: Merriam-Webster's dictionary defines sycophant as *a servile self-seeking flatterer*.

Thusia: This name is Greek for *sacrifice*. It is in the feminine. Both Thusia and Zebach whose names are connected allude to the deeper spiritual symbolism both characters represent echoing the meaning of sacrifice in a Judeo-Christian context.

Type Righter: Refer to the author's notes

AUTHOR'S NOTES:

It is true that each person reads out of their own experiential lens. As the author I respect that part of you, and what you as the reader bring to the table. I also am aware that readers appreciate when an author shares aspects of their writing that inspired it. For those of you who are taking the time to read this I feel led to share with you the identity of the type righter. This is probably one of the hardest aspects of an author's revelations because it involves exposing a very personal part of myself. I choose to share in hopes that my story will meet you in the continuum of what it means to be human.

The Type Righter was written as allegory of a year I chose to do deep emotional work for healing in my personal life. The process of writing was therapeutic, and life transforming. This perspective from which I understand and read the Type Righter makes my telling of it delicate at best. I am not sure I can unravel it all, but I can give a glimpse into that part I do understand.

The more that time goes by, I realize what is true. My work is a vehicle that expresses my unconscious self. The type righter character is an allegory of my unconscious being. As illustrated by Freud, most of an individual's life is guided by the unconscious, and like an iceberg, sits

151

mostly under the water. I have come to understand for my own life, emotional healing comes in the places where my unconscious self decides to live above the surface of the water. Writing has helped me do just that.

Allegorical characters that show up in the narrative either depict human relationships or other parts of my psyche that have played a role on my journey. I don't want to give them all away. You might recognize some of them in your own life. Once I have a chance to sit with my own story, and listen to it more closely, I may consider writing an analysis from an autobiographical perspective in the future.

I think the allegorical perspective applies to a psychological paradigm. The depiction of my healing journey is what I as an author felt compelled to share in a creative way. The healing process was both absorbed into my writing and in ways was a result of it. Understanding the power of my unconscious and how it affected my life was the foundation for my work.

On a larger scale, perhaps you as the reader can also apply allegory to the political, scientific, pharmaceutical, and technological influences of our time. To place the central theme of the book around a religious tone challenges the role that religion plays in world events. Perhaps how we choose to live in community has a connection with what prophesies come true in each generation. Hopefully the story makes us consider our future, and what kind of influence we want to make in the human experience. Thank you so much for your support of my work. I acknowledge your courage to face your own unconscious to bring a type of "rightness" for your own life.

-Rev. Dr. K. Helms

Bibliography

"A Quote by Friedrich Nietzsche." *Goodreads*. N.p.,n.d. Web. 05 Feb. 2017.

"BibleGateway." New International Version, New Living Translation (NIV, NLT)- Version Information-BibleGateway.com. N.p.,n.p. Web. 05 Feb. 2017.

"Coco J. Ginger Quotes (Author of The Way I Think of You)." *Coco J. Ginger Quotes*. N.p., n.p. Web. 05 Feb. 2017.

"Famous Quotes at BrainyQuote." *BrainyQuote*. Xplore, n.d. Web. 05 Feb. 2017.

Martinez, Nikki. "25 Quotes in the importance of Being Authentic." Huffington Post. N.p., 20 Dec. 2016. Web. 05 Feb. 2017.

Poe, Edgar Allan. *The Raven and Other Poems*. New York: Wiley and Putnam,1845. Print.

"Prime Time with Soledad O'Brian." *Essence*.May 2015. Web. 05 Feb. 2017.

"Quotes About Self (1824 Quotes)." *(1824 Quotes) N.p.,n.d. Web. 05 Feb. 2017.*